Deadly Ties

Jay Lang

Print ISBNs
Amazon Print 978-0-2286-2184-3
BWL Print 978-0-2286-2186-7
LSI Print 978-0-2286-2185-0
Ingram Spark 9780228627739

BWL Publishing

Books we love to write
Authors around the

http://bwlpublishing.ca

Dedication

To the memory of M. J. Young.
Forever with me in my heart.

Chapter One

As the door opened in the dead of night, I felt a rush of icy wind seconds before the killers appeared from the darkness.

* * *

A chilly morning wind gusts through the open car deck, almost causing me to lose my balance. Just as I reach the bottom of the metal stairwell, a distorted voice breaks through the overhead speakers. It's the captain, informing passengers that a pod of orca has been spotted off the starboard side.

Pushing against the wind, I make my way to the railing and look over the churning, grey water just in time to spot a large dorsal fin breaching the surface. Tourists quickly gather and shove to get the best vantage point for taking pictures.

After a few quick moments, the whales disappear and the onlookers slowly disperse. I lean over the railing and watch the whitecaps on the growing swells as we head into rougher seas. As the shorelines disappear, the wind picks up and mists of seawater spray over me. I continue to look out over the water, entranced by the pattern of the rolling waves. Though I get cold and wet from the saltwater spray, I don't return to my car until the Departure Bay dock comes into view.

The farther the ship gets from the mainland, the more apprehensive and resentful I feel about going back to a place I fought so hard to leave.

I haven't been home for a long time. I couldn't bear the thought of seeing him again, especially since Mom died. She was the go-between, the mediator between him and me. Over the years, I've opted for self preservation. Instead of visiting, I sent the obligatory card whenever a holiday or birthday rolled around. Yet, here I am in my late twenties, subjecting myself once more to the bullshit I escaped from.

The ferry docks, and as I drive over the noisy metal ramp onto solid ground, there's a sinking feeling in the pit of my gut.

I knew this day would eventually come. Years ago, when Mom was still alive, Dad was diagnosed with a carcinoid tumor in his lower intestine. From what his care nurse tells me, the cancer has now spread to his stomach and lungs, and as gruff and emotionally arrested as he is, I know my mom would've wanted me to help him in his final days.

Dark angry clouds hang overhead as a strong wind pushes against the body of my old Honda Accord, making it challenging to handle on the open highway. Despite this, the drive to Ladysmith goes by too quickly. Before I know it, I'm turning onto Brenton Page Road.

A few minutes down the road, I pull over so I can take a few steadying breaths. I remind myself that it's better to sacrifice time now than live with the guilt of not helping the cantankerous old codger.

I listen to a couple of Neil Young songs while gripping the steering wheel. Then, feeling as mentally prepared as I can, I pull back onto the road.

After I pass the tall white inn, I turn down the narrow, winding road toward the beach. When I come to the clearing, I see the half-dozen row of waterfront cabins just up from the shore. I park, get out of the car and stand, looking out over the sea.

When I was a child, I would wait until my mom was asleep, then I'd take off my clothes and tiptoe out to the beach. Standing naked under the stars by the glistening sea, the cool wind dancing around my body. It made me feel alive... a part of everything.

I couldn't do that now. I could never be that naked and vulnerable. Too much has made me feel self-conscious and ashamed. The freedom and purity I felt as a child was diminished by his strategic and calculating attempts to destroy me. Piece by piece, bit by bit he stole away the parts I needed to become a whole person.

But I wasn't the only one cut in half. My mother, God rest her, was a victim, same as me. It's why we needed each other so much. Together we made up a whole person.

I turn my attention to my father's cabin, which is shabbier than I remember— sun-bleached wood with cracked planks and a short walkway overgrown with weeds. The red paint on the door has faded to a dull burgundy, and the wooden chimes that I sent him a couple years ago are hanging crooked on a large, rusted hook.

I take a deep breath then rap twice on the door.

After a few long moments, I hear a gruff voice from inside the cabin. "Who is it?"

"It's me, Mila."

The latch unlocks and the door slowly opens. I barely recognize the man that looks back at me. My father, John Dovey, once nicknamed Grizzly for his broad and muscular physique, has become a withered and decrepit old man. He's thin and gangly, stooping forward in his wheelchair. If I had seen him anywhere but here, I wouldn't have recognized him.

He wheels backward, making room for the door to swing open so I can enter.

"Hi, Dad," I say, following him inside. His care-aids told me that he doesn't need the chair all the time. He can walk, just not for very long or very far.

"So, you finally decided to grace me with your presence," he slurs as he parks behind a rickety table, on which sits a half-bottle of whiskey and an empty glass.

I shut the door behind me and look around the small room. There's a worn-out green sofa that slouches in the middle where the springs have given way. His old rifle sits on a gun rack proudly displayed above the sofa. Pictures of my mom are hanging on the walls, along with a large corkboard covered with photos and post-it notes. The small gas stove and fridge have stains and dried food stuck to them. My father was never geared toward cleaning, something that drove my mother nuts.

"I wasn't sure you'd show," he says.

"Yeah, me either," I say in a low tone. "But we're family, so I didn't see where I had much choice."

"Family? Ha!" He grabs the bottle in his spindly, pale hand and shakes it at me. "You see this? This is the only damn family I got. The only family that's stood by me."

"That's brilliant, Dad. Spoken like a true reformed alcoholic."

"You can drop the sarcasm. It's beneath you."

I feel like saying, "No, quitting my job and giving up my life in Vancouver to care for a terminally ill, cantankerous alcoholic who's done his best to kill himself faster is beneath me" – but I don't. Instead, I shift my focus from him to the window, and try to compose myself.

He seems pissed off that I won't engage with him, grunting and pouring another drink. He sets the bottle down hard on the table. "I suppose you'll be needing to stay here."

Not on your life. "No, I called the manager of the cabins and asked if there were any vacancies. She said the cabin next door is opening up in a couple of days. Until then, I'll stay at the Inn up the road."

"What's the matter, don't wanna stay here with me? I wonder why that is?" He waves his arm around, spilling his drink. "Maybe you think you're too good because you've been living in the city. Ha! What a joke."

"You know, Dad." I glare at him. "It's not that I expected you to completely transform from the jerk you've always been, but I'd hoped you'd be a tiny bit happy to see me after five fucking years."

He stares at me, then smirks. "Not sure why you thought that. It's been years since you've darkened my door. You don't give a damn about me. You're probably waiting for me to die so you can take all my stuff."

A loud burst of laughter threatens to escape my lips. *Yeah, Dad, I left my peaceful life in Vancouver so I could finally get my hands on your rickety little table and nasty-ass couch. You found me out!*

I take a deep breath. "There's no point in talking. All we do is fight. I'm going to the inn, and I'll be back in the morning. Do you need anything?"

"Yeah, another one of these." He points to the bottle.

"Nice try." I walk to the door and turn the handle. "It would be nice if you were sober when I come back tomorrow."

He laughs. "For who?"

I walk outside and close the door behind me. *That sucked. Still, it could've been worse. At least he didn't throw anything at me.*

Just as I start toward the car, I hear my father yelling my name. I turn and open the door, poking my head in.

"What's up?"

He's still sitting with the drink in his hand. "Do you need any money?"

Taken aback, I shake my head. "I'm good. Thanks."

Chapter Two

I watch the small sailboats sway to the rhythm of the waves in the marina below as I debate going to the effort of ordering food. My room is one of six spa-like suites at the inn. I heard that a lot of writers would rent these rooms for months at a time when penning their next novel. Not surprising, considering the peaceful surroundings of the area.

I flop down on the bed and stare up at the ceiling, reflecting on the past forty-eight hours. The call from the medical supports that cared for my father, the disappointed reaction from my boss when I told him I was moving back to the Island, and—of course—the cold reunion with my father.

Feeling overwhelmed, like standing in the eye of a tornado with everything spinning out of control around me, my first instinct is to jump into my car and head back to my safe, peaceful life on the mainland. But I can't leave, and I know it. I'm bound here until my father's body gives out. My mother would be heartbroken if I left him to die alone, regardless that he's a raging alcoholic. My only option is to do what I can while staying emotionally distant and protected—yeah, right.

I order a pizza, then unpack my small suitcase into the chest of drawers. Then I go into the bathroom to freshen up.

I glance in the mirror. I look pale and stressed. When I left Vancouver this morning, I did a quick brush of my shoulder-length brown hair and tied it into a loose bun before dressing in leggings and an oversized hoodie—function over fashion, the same way I dress while babysitting all day. Now, after being to my father's place, I feel grungy and gross.

* * *

The first blast of morning sun breaks over the horizon and casts a blinding light through the large windows. I turn over and throw my arm over my eyes. For a brief moment, I think I'm home in Vancouver, and then reality hits me.

I roll onto my back and force in a deep full breath, then exhale slowly. I can't believe I'm actually here, just minutes away from him. I must be out of my fucking mind.

I sit up and swing my legs over the edge of the bed. My life in Vancouver has ended, at least for now. I need to put on my big-girl panties and accept it.

My phone rings on the way to the bathroom. It's the supervisor for the company that provides in-home care for my father.

I listen patiently as she relays the many incidents that care aids endured while caring for my dad. She drops words like *abusive, alcoholic,* and *unstable.* All I can think is, *no shit, lady, try growing up with him.*

She then suggests putting Dad into palliative care. I humor her and agree, knowing there's no chance in hell my father would ever leave his cabin for a regulated place that doesn't allow alcohol.

I assure the woman that I'll be taking care of him from now on, apologize for the trouble he's caused, and thank her for her service. As she says goodbye, I can tell by her tone how relieved she is to be done with his bullshit.

Just before she hangs up, she informs me that all his care aids have heard my father speak of me with pride and adoration. I snicker to myself. They obviously weren't aware of my father's tendency towards sarcasm.

After getting dressed, I head out of the inn and drive into town.

Ladysmith is a quaint little bedroom community with a big portion of the population made up of retirees. Being only an hour from Victoria, a lot of the businesses

14

here rely on tourism to supplement the economy.

Once in town, I stop by a local coffee shop, grab a latte, and find a seat. A few laid-back patrons are scattered throughout the small shop. When I glance at them, they look back and smile, something I've grown unaccustomed to while living in Vancouver. In the city, people are stand-offish and typically focussed on an electronic device. Here, there's a strong sense of community and connection. I never realized how much I missed that aspect of living in a small town until now.

I grab a local paper from an adjacent table and flip to the classifieds. If I'm going to be living here, I'll have to find a job. While sipping my coffee, I scan the help wanted ads. There are many listings for yard work, handyman jobs and one ad for a cab driver.

I slide my phone out of my pocket and snap a picture of the contact information for the taxi driver job. Then I take the last sip from my cup and am just about to leave when an elderly gentleman with a grey comb-over and pop-bottle glasses walks up to my table.

"Hi, Miss," he says in a soft voice. "You finished with my paper yet?"

"Your paper?" I repeat, feeling embarrassed. "I'm so sorry. I didn't realize it belonged to someone. I just thought I'd search the classifieds really quickly." I offer the paper.

He laughs. "It's ok. I set it down at my usual table then walked away." He gently takes the paper from my hand. "Did you find what you were looking for?"

I smile. "A job. I was scanning the job listings."

"And?"

"And I'm not sure. The only job that might be something I could do is cab driving."

"Ah, yes," he says. "My nephew owns the cab company here. He needs to hire someone quickly because one of his drivers up and quit." The man leans in closer to me. "The guy had to leave on account of his health."

"Oh no. Was he sick?"

"He was messing around with another driver's wife and got found out."

I shake my head and laugh. Typical small town. Everyone knows what you've done before you've got your pants up.

"What's your name?" he asks.

"Mila."

"Pleased to meet you, Mila. I'm Rupert." He pulls out his phone. "Tell you what. Why don't I give my nephew a call and see if he can meet with you?"

"Really?" I say, taken aback.

"Of course!" Rupert stands close as he dials a number on his cell phone, then loudly converses with the person on the other end. By the time he's finished, the other patrons are pretty much up to date on the fact that I'm unemployed and Rupert is doing my bidding for me.

When the call finally ends, he smiles confidently and tells me that his nephew can see me now, if I have a few minutes to spare. "The office is only a ten-minute walk from here."

I thank Rupert for his kindness and head out of the cafe, my head whirling.

This would never happen to me in the city. Although I'm completely unprepared, no resume, underdressed and not in the right mind frame to sell myself, I know that an opportunity like this won't present itself twice.

* * *

The old guy was right—it took less than ten minutes to get to the small, stand-alone cab company on White Street.

Rupert's nephew, Don, is sitting behind a cluttered long desk with a laptop opened in front of him. He's about forty-five and has a thin comb-over resembling Rupert's. He knows my name before I even open my mouth and motions for me to sit in a chair in the corner of the small room. Usually, I would feel over-wrought with nerves in a job interview, but here in this humble little office, sitting with a guy that could pass for a used car salesman or someone in the custodial arts, I am at ease.

Don and I talk for a half-hour about what brings me to Ladysmith, how long I'm staying, and what would make me a good cab driver. I give him a sweetened-up answer to every question he asks, assuring him that I have a perfect driving record and a class 4 licence from when I drove a limo in the city a few summers ago. By the end of the interview, Don is smiling and passing me a map of the area, disregarding the bit I told him about growing up here, and suggests I study it before starting my first shift in two days.

I push aside my enthusiasm over getting a job and slowly walk back to my car, dreading the inescapable visit with my dad. With some luck, I'll find out how he's getting his booze every day, but I highly doubt he'll reveal his supplier. My guess is that he picks up the phone and calls a local bootlegger that survives off chronic drinkers like my father.

Then I remind myself that I'm not here to cure my father. My intentions are much more selfish than that. I'm waiting for him to die.

Not because of the pain and strife that he's caused my mother and me, but for the simple reason that his declining health isn't just the by-product of his cancer—it's the end result of his quest to self-destruct. If anything, I have to give my father kudos for being committed. Be it from guilt, self-loathing, or resentment, he swam to the bottom of a bottle and hasn't resurfaced since Mom died. Maybe his terminal diagnosis could've been staved off if he had the balls to quit drinking.

My perspective would've brought on great opposition from my mother, a tolerant wife who always made excuses for her husband. It always enraged me. When my dad came home from a night of binge drinking, belligerent and staggering, he'd go to work on me first, ensuring that my self-esteem was just as he left it: bruised and insignificant. A few coarse words and a random cuff to the head usually did the trick. When he was satisfied with the damage to me, he'd focus on my mother. Every time, she'd only combat his words with a soft, gentle tone of reason.

It never worked. Alcohol was just an accelerant to his already fractured character. From what Mom told me, he had been raised by alcoholic parents. He was imprinted with abuse and never found enough strength to change it. If it wasn't for the love of my mother, my interpretation of a healthy parent-child relationship would've been pretty fucked.

Still, I've never had what could be classified as a functional relationship with anyone. My feelings were always too fear-based, which is never a good foundation for building trust. Every relationship ended the same way, with the girl saying I was suffocating her with my trust issues. On occasion, they suggested I seek counselling to help me deal with my emotional problems.

In my defense, I didn't attract the most honorable of women. The girls I chose always lived fast and shunned commitment. No matter how hard I tried to change the type of girl that I was normally drawn to, they all turned out to be the same inside.

Chapter Three

Over the next couple days, my time is spent running around for my father, getting his groceries and meds, and cleaning his place. Whenever I have a spare moment, I study the new street map of the area.

We scoff at each other a few times, but nothing out-of-control. He doesn't say much that means he gives a damn, certainly nothing equalling a congratulations over me finding employment so quickly.

Fortunately, I spent my last night at the hotel and can move into my own cabin today. I won't have to run back and forth from the inn anymore. By a stroke of luck, I meet the old tenants while moving in. They have a brown leather sofa, a recliner, and a kitchen table they don't want to take, so I offer a few bucks and it's a done deal. Saves me a lot of time and money. Yesterday I picked up a blanket and a pillow, so for now I don't have to worry about a bed. I can just crash on the couch.

I'm completely settled in by 4PM, an hour before I have to be at the cab company for my first shift. I take a fast shower, tie my hair into a loose bun, slide on black slacks and a sweater, and head out.

* * *

Don shows me the cab—a Chevy Lumina that looks more like an old cop car than a taxi—then gives me a quick rundown of how the navigation system works on the computer screen fixed to the dash. In the few minutes before my shift starts, I buzz into a nearby coffee spot to grab an espresso and a handful of snacks to keep me going through the night.

My evening starts pretty uneventfully: an elderly lady going from the mall to a nearby apartment, a teen girl returning home after babysitting all day, and two ladies in their fifties off to test their luck at bingo. Every passenger is super friendly and talkative, which settles my first-day nerves.

As I wait for the next call, I idle on the roadside so I can eat a snack and phone Dad.

He's slurring and ranting about something on TV that pissed him off. After making a bullshit excuse to end the call, I say that I'll swing by in the morning. He grumbles and hangs up.

I polish off the last bite of my muffin just as Don messages me about another fare. A bus stop, not far from the highway.

En route, it starts to rain. By the time I reach the stop, the sprinkle has turned into a full-on downpour, and my wipers are on high-speed.

Pulling close to the stop, I strain to make out the willowy figure in the darkness. It's a woman with a large suitcase, two shoulder bags, and a guitar case at her feet.

I park next to the small plexiglass shelter and slide down the window. "Did you order a cab?"

Her long, blond hair is stuck to her skin, obstructing most of her face. She nods before fumbling with her bags. I pop the trunk and hop out, getting instantly soaked. Quickly, I help the girl pack the large suitcase in the trunk.

Once it's loaded, the girl clambers into the backseat with the rest of her bags and I slide behind the wheel.

"Wow, that's a lot of baggage to be hauling on the bus," I say, starting the car.

She laughs. "Tell me about it." Her voice is soft and unassuming. "I was on my way to a gig. My car broke down. Had to call a tow truck."

"Where were you heading?"

She lets out a frustrated sigh. "The Joker Lounge here in town. I wasn't planning on bringing everything I own with me. Or looking like a drowned rat."

"I'm sorry about your car." I try to get a glimpse of her face in the rear-view mirror. "Are you from out of town?"

"Victoria, on the rare occasion I don't have a gig. Otherwise, I stay in hotels in whatever town I'm playing."

"That's great. Do you just play guitar? Or do you sing as well?"

"Both."

The cab passes under a streetlight and I catch a glimpse of the drenched stranger in the back seat. Captivating green eyes shine out from behind wet, blond locks.

As we drive toward First Street, I steal the odd glance. Her lips are naturally pink and stand out against her porcelain skin. She looks to be the same age as me— somewhere in her late twenties. The soft edges of her face remind me of a flawless portrait hanging in a gallery. She is perfect.

Before I had clearly seen her, my words came easy. Now, knowing how stunning this creature is, my hands begin to sweat and I fumble for my words.

Before I know it, we're pulling onto First Street and only a couple of blocks from The Joker Lounge. The hard rain has reduced to a drizzle, making it easier to read the marquees and signs on the buildings.

"What's your name?"

I glance in the mirror, relieved we're not face-to-face. "Mila. Yours?"

I watch as the edges of her full lips turn upward. "Ava."

Knowing I only have a couple minutes before she exits the cab and disappears forever, I muster my bravery and ask, "What are you going to do with your luggage while you play?"

"I have no idea. I was planning on getting a room before my gig, but the car wasted so much time. I've only got half an hour before my first set." Those green eyes meet mine. "Why do you ask?"

"I...uh..." I swallow hard. "If you need a ride to a hotel after you're finished, you can leave your bags in the trunk. You can call me when you're done, and I can give you a ride. I mean...If you want."

She's quiet for a moment. "You're very kind. I just might take you up on that. If you're sure it's not too much trouble?"

"It's fine. I don't think any passengers will need to use the trunk tonight. Unless they're disposing a body, in which case I'll just cram it on top of your suitcase."

She says nothing, and instantly I feel a wave of regret for spewing out the lame joke.

Then: "Please don't do that," she says seriously. "Do you know how hard it is to get corpse smell out of fabric? I can tell you from experience—it's a real bitch."

Our eyes meet in the mirror and we simultaneously bust out laughing.

I pull up to the glowing red sign of The Joker Lounge. Ava fumbles with her things in the backseat for a few moments.

"So, any idea what time you'd like me to come back tonight?"

"The lounge is only open till ten. I'll call you through the dispatch."

She steps out of the car, then turns to grab her bags. She swings them over one shoulder and hoists the guitar case in the other hand.

Before she closes the back door, she leans down and looks over the seat at me. "Thanks for doing this. I'll let you know if they boo me off early. I just hope I have enough time to get fixed up."

"It's no trouble. And don't worry—you could wear a gunnysack with your hair sticking straight up and you'd still look great."

As soon as the words leave my lips, I regret it. I sound like a desperate pervert. My face flushes.

She flashes a perfect smile. "Thank you."

* * *

For the next few hours of picking up and dropping off passengers, all I can think of is Ava.

The evening passes in a haze, and to my shock I see that it's nearing ten. Though I'm not tired, I stop by a drive-thru for a coffee, just for something to occupy my brain while I wait.

I'm just taking the last sip when the computer screen lights up and the address for the Joker Lounge appears on the screen. Immediately, my hands clam up.

She looks different than she did hours ago. Her hair is a flowing, golden blond, and her pale skin now has some color. Wearing a tight pair of jeans and a black suit jacket with matching boots, she looks fashionable and hot.

She opens the back door of the cab and puts her bags and guitar case on the seat. Then, to my shock, she slides into the passenger seat next to me.

As soon as she closes the door, the gentle aroma of lavender fills the car. She clicks her seatbelt in and looks over at me. "Thanks for keeping my suitcase safe."

"It's nothing, really." I smile without making eye contact. "Where am I taking you?"

She has a reservation at the motel just off the highway. It's a ways away, which suits me fine. On the trip, she asks me how long I've been in the area. I briefly touch on why I'm in Ladysmith, giving her the rosy version.

Ava tells me how she doesn't stay in one place long enough to call it home. More often than not, she lives out of her suitcase at motels up and down the Island. She's getting tired of being on the road, but she's been performing for years and has no idea what else she could do. I tell her that she sounds articulate and bright, and I'm sure she'd do fine in anything she put her mind to.

My statement makes her blush, and she reaches over and lightly pushes my shoulder. "You don't know me. Maybe I'm a sociopath and I'm manipulating you into thinking good things about me."

"You could be right. I've definitely been wrong about people in the past. Especially women."

Ava chuckles, then points ahead to the old, blue motel on the side of the road.

After I pull up to the entrance, Ava reaches into her bag, unearths a few bills, and places them on the dash. "Thanks again, Mila."

I get out and retrieve her suitcase from the trunk. As I place it on the ground, I notice the name *A. Fellows* on the tag.

Her hands are full with her guitar and smaller bags, so I follow her to the lobby door with the suitcase.

"I'm good from here," she says with a smile, hooking an arm through a bag handle so she can grab the suitcase. "Are you working tomorrow evening?"

"No. I work the following afternoon. Why?"

Ava looks down at her feet. "I just thought that maybe…if you were free…you'd like to catch one of my sets at the lounge. I'm here for two more nights."

I laugh. "If I'm bored?"

"Yeah, or whatever."

"I'll come, but not because I'll be bored. It'd be cool to watch you play."

She asks for my number, and I watch her punch it into her phone.

With that, Ava walks inside the building and I get back into the cab. My head filled with the beautiful stranger, I drive back to headquarters to conclude my first interesting day on the job.

Chapter Four

I wake to my phone ringing beside me. As soon as I see the number on the screen, I tense up—it's my father. What a way to start the day.

I take a deep breath and prepare for the undoubted bitching and moaning I'll have to listen to. On the off chance the purpose of his call is of a medical nature, I don't ignore the call completely. After a quick trip to the bathroom and a few sips of water, I return his call.

"Hello."

Immediately, I detect the booze in his voice. "Dad. What's up?"

"What's up? What's up? What a stupid question."

I turn and look out the window. The rays of the morning sun dance off the calm water. The shoreline is brushed with a soft, pinkish hue. I've got to repel the poison coming at me over the phone. I can't let him influence, control, and ruin my day.

"Dad, I don't have long. Tell me what you need so I can get on with my day."

"Ha! All about you, huh? Your day. What you gotta do. What's so important, anyway? I thought you came here to take care of me!"

"Yes, I'm here to help you. But I'm trying to set up my own place. I need to find a bed."

"Waste of money! Just sleep on the couch, that's what I do. You don't need a bed, unless you're planning on having company over." He laughs. "You still like girls?"

"Not as much as you like whiskey," I blurt out, momentarily losing control.

I wait for it—for him to think of his next cutting line—but it doesn't come.

"Dad, are you managing to eat?"

"Yeah, the damn delivery driver dropped off my meals this morning. That's another thing. They show up too bloody early. Make them come later in the day."

Why is that, Dad? Too hungover in the morning to answer the door?

Just to appease him, I agree to call the meal delivery company. Then I assure him I'll be over to grab his laundry this afternoon, and I can finally hang up.

* * *

There's a mattress shop in town, on Roberts Street. The salesclerk is in her mid-forties and has a sunny disposition. She's not pushy and aggressive like some of the competitive salesclerks in the city, and she makes sure I'm completely satisfied when I choose a bed from the showroom floor. I leave the shop clutching the paperwork, relieved that soon I'll be sleeping on a proper bed.

After a morning of spending too much money in different shops, I head back to the cabins to tend to my father.

I rap on his door and wait for what seems like forever until he yells for me to come in. He's sitting on the sofa, an open box on the cushion beside him.

"Hi, Dad. How are you?"

"I'm great. Just living the dream."

I chuckle. "Is that right?"

"How was your first night driving cab?"

I'm shocked by his question. Feeling suspicious, I wait for him to add something derogatory. He doesn't. Instead, he leans over and pulls the box onto his knees.

"You need help putting that box away?" I ask.

"Why the hell would I need help?"

"Never mind." I look around the room for dirty laundry.

"Come and sit with me for a minute," he orders.

I walk over and sit on the far end of the couch.

It's only when I see him reach into the box that I notice how badly his hands are shaking. I remember that alcoholism isn't his only issue. Cancer is also kicking the shit out of him.

"Do you remember when I bought you this?" He pulls out a ratty white bunny with a missing eye.

"Where did you find him?" I grab the stuffy and examine it. "I thought he got lost when I was ten."

"You left him on the beach. After we moved, I went back and found him. I assumed you'd outgrown him, so I stuffed him in a box for safekeeping."

I feel a lump form in my throat, and I fight back the emotion—not because he kept the toy for me, but because I can't believe he cared enough to search for it.

"Thanks, Dad." I run my finger over the bunny's ears.

He then pulls a picture of Mom and me from the box that, just the other day, had been hanging on the wall. I turn to see a perfectly clean square, where the picture protected the wall from discoloring.

He holds the picture out to me. "I thought you could hang it in your new place."

I take the picture from him, wondering why he's being so generous. My first thought is that he received a call from his doctor when I wasn't here. "Dad, is there something you're not telling me? Do you know something I don't?"

He looks at me briefly. "Of course I know something you don't! I know a lot of things you don't."

And with that, he takes the last item out of the box. It's a book, and right away I recognize the black shaggy dog on the cover. In bold letters is the title, *Black Dog Dream Dog*, a book my mother would read to me over and over.

He hands it over. I hold it in my lap, and as I look at the cover, I can hear her voice as she made each character her own.

"Your mother saved it for you," he says. "I would've given it to you sooner, but you never came to visit."

A hot tear rolls down my cheek, and I quickly brush it away before he notices.

He pushes the box onto the floor. "Now that's done, I need a bloody drink."

"Yeah." I put the items carefully in my bag and stand. "I should really get your laundry and take off. I've got a ton of things to take care of today."

"Well, get to it, then. And remember to call the meal delivery bastards. If those little no-minds show up early again, I'm meeting them at the door with my gun!"

* * *

After dropping the treasures off at my cabin, I drive to the laundromat with my and my father's dirty clothes. It's one shitty thing about living in the cabins—no laundry machines.

At least I'll have something clean to wear tonight. I feel a wave of excitement and anxiety as I load the washing machines. In just a few short hours, I'll be at the Lounge, watching Ava perform.

After turning on the machines, I sit on a hard plastic chair and reach for the local paper beside me. When I glance at the cover, the headline jumps off the page: *Ladysmith Sees Increasing Number of Drug Houses in Once Safe Residential Neighbourhoods.*

I feel both sad and disgusted. Ladysmith has always felt safe and free from the criminal element that plagues more populated places, like Nanaimo or Victoria. I can't imagine what the local long-time residents are feeling. Invaded to some degree, I'm sure.

After perusing the bulk of the paper, I flip through the last few pages and stop when I see an ad for The Joker Lounge. There's a *Now Appearing* headline, with a picture of a girl beneath.

It's her. Ava.

The crappy, reprinted photo makes it hard to see her face clearly, but below it is her name: Ava Fellows. Vocals and guitar. I glance around to make sure no one was watching, then rip the ad from the page. After gently folding it, I stuff the picture into my pocket.

My mind floods with the memory of her in the backseat. Wet hair, shockingly green eyes.

For a moment, the breathlessness I felt in that moment rushes back to me. Then, the washing machine makes a horrid buzzing sound, snapping me out of my daydream.

* * *

When I drop Dad's laundry off, he's half lit. His already less-than-desirable mood has dipped into slurring, negative rants. His borderline kindness from the morning is miles away.

When I finally get back to my place, my anxiety doubles. Soon, I'll be seeing Ava again. And she'll be seeing me.

I rummage desperately through my outfits, trying to find something more edgy and less dull than what she saw me in last.

After a long, frustrating hour, I piece together a pair of black jeans, short rocker boots, and a Pink Floyd concert shirt. After brushing my hair and adding some rouge to my cheeks and mascara to my lashes, I'm ready to go—at least, on the outside.

On the drive to the lounge, I take slow, deep breaths and tell myself that there's no need to be nervous. Ava is just a person like me. No better, no worse.

And why am I so nervous anyway? It's not like I'm going with the hopes of her being into me. She probably doesn't even like girls.

Oh, please like girls…

The room is small, with a half-dozen crowded tables in front of the small platform stage, lit only with pods in the ceiling. A short, mahogany bar with a bald man bartending is at the end of the room.

With no sign of Ava, I maneuver around the tables to the bar and sit on the only available stool. After ordering a ginger ale, I ask the bartender when Ava is due to play.

"Anytime now!" he says brightly. Like most of the locals, he's outgoing and talkative, and goes on about how great Ava's previous performance was. "Hence the crowd," he finishes, sweeping an arm to indicate the packed house.

The crowd suddenly gets louder, and I turn to see a blond, statuesque figure with a guitar climbing onto the small stage. My heart beats faster.

As Ava positions herself on the stool, she crosses her long legs, tightening the black mini skirt over her shapely thighs. The blouse she's wearing is a white, light cotton, and unbuttoned to show her long, swan-like neck.

The murmurs of conversation quiet when the first chord rings out. Folk music—I love it.

Her voice is soulful and captivating. No heads turn away as she plays. My eyes are locked onto the way her fingers move, the way her hair catches the stage light. She is perfect.

At the end of the first song, she greets everyone kindly and thanks them for coming out. I can tell she's self-conscious. Her voice doesn't show it, but I can tell by the way her eyes address the room without focussing on one individual. For some reason, it makes her even more irresistible.

After a half-dozen songs, she sets the guitar against the wall and walks toward the bar. Toward me. My throat is suddenly very dry, and I quickly take a slug of my ginger ale.

People stop her along the way, giving her accolades for her performance, which she accepts graciously. Finally, she reaches the bar. She orders a pop, then turns to me. "You showed." She smiles. "I'm happy you did."

My mouth is instantly dry again, but I don't take a sip of my drink. I'm worried about my hands trembling as I raise the glass to my lips.

"You sounded amazing," I say instead. Thankfully, my voice doesn't crack.

She looks everywhere but my eyes. "Thanks. I wasn't sure if folk was something you'd be into."

"Are you kidding me?" I scoff. "It's all I listen to. I have a Neil Young CD in my car on permanent rotation."

Finally, her green eyes meet mine, just briefly. But just as she goes to speak, a middle-aged woman comes up to talk to her. Then another, and another, until Ava's break has been taken up by eager fans.

She nudges her drink toward me. "Sorry—can you keep an eye on this while I do my next set?"

"Of course." I watch her push through the crowd toward the stage. Though I didn't get a lot of her undivided attention during her break, I feel grateful for the attention I did get. Those green eyes on mine.

Ava takes her seat and pulls her guitar onto her lap. Just before she starts to play, she looks at the audience. "This next song goes out to Mila, a new friend."

As soon as she plays the first couple chords, I recognize the song. Neil Young's "Harvest Moon." One of my faves.

I watch, listen, and applaud as she perfectly performs her next set. When she's finished, she grabs her guitar and walks back over to the bar.

In between interruptions from the odd fan, we steal bits of conversation about our tastes in music, her preference for playing cover songs, and how she likes trying out original music in front of a live audience.

Eventually, people filter out of the lounge and the bartender starts wiping down tables.

Ava looks up at a Pilsner sign with a clock on it above the bar. "I guess we should go. The lounge closes soon and the nightclub next door opens."

Outside, folks are lining up to get inside the nightclub. I turn to face Ava. "Do you want to get a coffee somewhere?"

"I'd love to, but I've got to figure out my car."

"Do you know what's wrong with it?"

"Yeah. Kind of a crappy scenario. It's the transmission."

I give her a sympathetic look. "I'm sorry. That sucks."

"Oh well." She shrugs. "There's always worse things."

"That's a great attitude. And you're right."

"Are you heading home?"

I grin. "Yeah, I've got nowhere else to be."

"Do you think I could catch a ride with you to my motel, if it's not out of your way?"

"Absolutely."

On the short walk across the parking lot, I become increasingly aware of just how dated my Honda is. As we approach the car, I feel the need to defend myself. "Excuse my less-than-lux car. I only use it as a puddle jumper in the city."

She laughs. "Don't be silly. At least it runs."

From the time I start the car to when I pull up in front of the motel, we don't stop talking once.

"Thanks for the lift," she says, opening the door. "I'm in Ladysmith until they fix my car, so if you've got free time, would you want to hang out?"

"Well, truth is, I've been picking up a kind of weird girl, stranger danger vibe off you. Yeah, I'm not so sure I wanna chance it."

"You're a jerk." She laughs. "If you're going to be up later, I'll give you a call."

I nod. "Sounds great."

I check in on Dad before going home, which is a huge mistake—he's slumped over the table and yelling into his glass. As long as he's not injured or unconscious, there's not much I can do about it. I quietly close the door.

I make a quick meal and just as I'm tidying up, Ava calls. "I just ordered a large pizza," she says the moment I pick up. "I'm intent on polishing off the entire thing."

I laugh in amazement at how someone so lanky can eat so much.

During the course of the night, we talk about everything, no holds barred. I'm not sure what it is—something about her makes me feel free to express myself. With girls in the past, I felt vulnerable disclosing certain things. Not with Ava. I want to tell her everything and, at the same time, learn everything about her. I don't feel like I'm being judged.

Without asking her directly, I discover that she's gay, or at least bi. She mentions dating a girl a few months ago, and how they broke up when Ava caught her doing drugs. She abhors drugs. I talk about my mom dying, then about my father's raging alcoholism and terminal cancer.

I can tell she feels bad for me. Not exactly the reaction I was going for.

"Were you close to him when you were a child?" she asks.

"Not really. We didn't see him much when I was growing up. He would blow into town every six months and throw a wad of cash on the table, and just as we were getting used to having him around again, he'd get a call from some frozen, far away place and he'd be gone.

"My mother, my everything, used to romanticize it—me without a father, her without a husband—by saying that because he's gone so much, we'd never get tired of him. We'd always eagerly await the next time he'd walk through the door. I bought none of it. My father was an introvert who had no interest in sharing his attentions with anyone. Being a mine inspector was a perfect fit. Other than meeting workers on-site, he spent most of his time confined to a tiny bunkhouse room.

"I knew he drank, even when I was young. When he was at home, he'd pull out a bottle after hours of listening to Mom and me give him updates on what happened while he was away. It wasn't until after he'd hit rock bottom that he actually started communicating with us. Mom even got him to quit drinking and attend AA meetings, which she of course attended as well, for moral support. He was lucky to have her. We both were."

I realize then how long I'd been ranting. "Are you still there? Or did I put you to sleep?"

"Of course, I'm still here." There was a pause. "I'm really sorry about your mom passing. It sounds like she held everything together."

"Yeah, she did," I say with a sigh. "But now that I spewed everything at you, tell me more about you as a kid. All I know so far is that you spent a lot of time around Victoria. Do you have siblings? Family?"

"No parents. I mean, not anymore. I did, of course, until they passed away."

"Are you serious? You lost both of your parents? I am so sorry." I feel like a jerk for bringing it up.

She laughs. "Don't sweat it. It was a long time ago."

"I can't imagine what you've been through."

"Of course you can. You lost your mom, and now your father is terminally ill. You know what it's like."

I realize that she's right. "I guess. And no siblings? Me either."

"No, I have a sister. She's a year older than me."

"Oh, really? Tell me about her."

Ava suddenly yawns. "My God, it's 3 AM. I'm bushed, aren't you? We should probably hit the sack. But I'm around tomorrow, if you wanna get together."

"Yeah, sure. That would be great." I have a sneaking suspicion that my question about her sister prompted this abrupt end to the call. "I work in the afternoon, but only until nine. Did you want to get together after that? I can pick you up after my shift."

"That would be great."

It takes me a long time to fall asleep. Even if the couch wasn't lumpy, my mind wouldn't turn off—it's full of Ava. I toss and turn through what's left of the night, and when I finally, briefly close my eyes, a loud rap sounds at the door and my eyes fly open to a bright, sunny room.

Slowly, I focus enough to stand and stagger to the door. Two young men in their late teens are standing on the stoop, one with a clipboard in his hands.

"Hi. We're here to deliver your bed."

Blearily I peer outside and see a cube van, the mattress store logo on the side.

* * *

One bed setup and three coffee's later, I'm finally alert and have my second wind in time for my shift. Thankfully it's busy, which keeps me from losing steam and passing out at the wheel.

Three out of the dozen or so passengers bring up the subject of drug houses, expressing their rage about how nothing is being done to eradicate the problem. Trying to be the realist, I gently explain how law enforcement is probably doing all they can, but it's hard to know the ins and outs of every dealer, regardless of how small the town is. My words fall on deaf ears. They're used to having a safe community and, in their minds, the police are at fault. I'm definitely not looking for arguments, so I do what I've been hired to do: be friendly and drive them to their destinations. That's all.

Finally, my shift ends. I decide to call Ava and see if she's free, so I don't drive all the way home, only to turn around and come back to town.

She answers on the first ring. Her voice sounds higher, and I pick up stress in her tone. "Hey. How are you?"

"Pissed off. I have been freaking all day."

"Why? What's up?"

She goes on about how the transmission for her car won't get here for days. "And then there's the installation—who knows how long that'll take. There's no way I have the cash to pay for my room that long, especially considering how much the damn garage is charging."

"I can see why you're stressed. What are you going to do?"

"I don't know. I guess I can go back to Victoria, but I'd have to call around, see if any friends are going to be around."

I can't believe I'm doing this, after only knowing her for a couple days, but something about her tells me to go for it. "Ava, this is going to sound a little off the wall, but...you could stay at my place until your car is fixed."

I hold my breath, waiting for her reply.

There are a few long beats before she answers. "Are you kidding me?"

"I know. Random, right? I wasn't trying to freak you out, I just thought–"

"I'm not freaked out. I'm just surprised you'd offer when I'm almost a stranger to you."

"I'm surprised too," I say with a giggle. "Then again, sometimes you have to trust your gut."

"I completely agree." There's a pause. "And I would love to crash at your place. But I insist on giving you a few bucks, paying for my food, etcetera."

"Sounds good." My face feels very warm. "Just so you're not disappointed, I should tell you that I live in a cabin by the water. There's no five-star lodging happening over here."

"Are you kidding? That sounds perfect!"

Chapter Five

I've got two hours to make sure everything is clean and tidy before I pick Ava up. After wiping everything down—twice—the rustic little cabin looks about as good as I can get it. Thankfully, I don't have to work until this evening, so I can spend time getting her settled before I leave.

On my way to pick up Ava, I check in on Dad. He's lying on the couch with a bucket on the floor beside him, and doesn't let out any of his usual snide comments when I enter, which makes me worry a bit. He tells me he's nauseated due to the meal he had earlier, but I suspect it's something more.

I decide to wait and see how he feels tomorrow. If he's not feeling better by then, I'll call his doctor.

* * *

The midday sun softly illuminates the streets that were saturated in darkness and rain just hours ago. I wait outside the old blue motel, nerves fluttering.

A minute after I'd texted her my arrival, she struggles with her bags through the lobby door. I quickly get out and run to her side, grabbing a couple of her bags.

After we've fit all her gear in my car, she slides into the passenger seat and looks over at me with a big smile. "I'm so grateful to you for offering your place."

There's nothing on her face showing any misgivings or regrets about crashing at the cabin with me. I breathe a sigh of relief and start the car.

Over the drive, after the town centre fades in the rear-view, Ava expresses amazement at the scenery changes of tall, green firs lining the road. When we reach the cabins, she gets out of the car and looks out over the sea.

"It's like I'm standing in a moving painting," she says. "It's spectacular here."

I hope her excitement doesn't diminish too much when she sees the inside of my small, rustic cabin.

After we unload her gear into the living room, it takes about ten seconds to show her the place. I can tell by the way her face shines that I don't have to worry about her excitement diminishing.

"I love it," she says simply.

I tell her that she can move her things into the bedroom and I'll take the couch. She argues with me, not wanting to put me out of my room. I manage to convince her, and she gratefully concedes before hauling her things into my bedroom.

With Ava here, the last thing I want is to go to work. I'd rather chill out and talk and order take-out. Unfortunately, I'm new on the job. It's not like I can ask someone to fill in for me.

We talk for what seems like a few minutes, until I look at the clock and realize that it's been a couple hours. With regret, I head out the door.

* * *

I stop in to see my father before heading downtown. Thankfully, he's feeling spryer than last night. He's eaten, kept his food down, and is back to his normal self—angrily bitching about politicians and how they're ruining the country.

My shift runs smoothly but slowly. My mind is completely focussed on Ava, wondering if she's comfortable and feels at home in the cabin.

When my shift ends, I walk into the taxi-stand to turn in the cab keys.

"You're getting a bit of a break," Don says, taking the keys. "Another driver of mine needs some extra shifts, so you can take the weekend off. You'll start an evening shift on Monday."

Wanting him to think I'm an eager employee, I sigh with fake disappointment over not being on the schedule for the next couple of days. In reality, I'm nothing but thrilled about having the next few days free with Ava.

* * *

As soon as I open the door to my place, I'm hit with a waft of lavender, along with the smell of soy sauce and ginger. Ava is standing in the kitchen, holding two plates of what looks like Chinese food.

"Hi," I say, smiling and walking over. "You cooked?"

She snorts. "Yeah, right." She motions to the silver take-out containers in the garbage. "Trust me. You don't want me to cook."

Over dinner, we briefly talk about my uneventful day before lapsing into a comfortable silence. She looks around as we eat, her expression soft.

"You know," she says. "This cabin reminds me of when Mom and Dad would take me to visit my grandmother on Salt Spring Island."

"Really?"

"Yeah. She lived in a cottage close to the beach, just like this."

"Does she still?" I ask, lifting a forkful of noodles to my mouth.

Ava shakes her head. "She passed when I was twelve. Long battle with cancer."

Again, I feel awful. Me and my big mouth. "I'm sorry. It's never easy to lose a loved one. I'm glad your parents took you to stay with her when they did."

"Yeah." Ava pokes at her food, not looking at me. "That's when they had their shit together."

"Had their shit together? What do you mean?"

Ava takes a deep breath. "They got into drugs pretty heavily later on. It's what ended up killing them."

It's a moment before I can respond. "I don't know what to say."

She shrugs. "There's not much you can say. Besides, they knew what they were doing. They chose to slide down that rabbit hole, leaving my sister and me to fend for ourselves."

"How old were you when they died?"

"I was fourteen. My sister was fifteen. My mom overdosed first. Then it was my dad's turn, six months later."

"And you and your sister were left all alone?"

"Yes and no. We got put into a foster home. But believe me, we would've fared a lot better on the street."

She goes on to describe a horrible situation where her foster parents drank every night and abused Ava and her sister. How the foster family was evicted due to complaints from neighbours about loud

52

parties. How when her sister turned seventeen, she landed a live-in babysitting job in Campbell River, where she took Ava for a couple of years. "After that ended, we worked odd jobs up and down the Island. It was hard, but we got through it."

I put my hand on hers. "I can't believe how strong you are for surviving on your own at such a young age."

"I don't feel strong. You just do what you have to."

I nod, amazed still. "And your sister? Where is she now?"

It takes ten solid seconds for her to answer. "Jail."

Shocked, I accidentally drop my fork. It makes a loud *ting* as it hits the plate. "Wow," is all I can say.

"Yeah," she says in a soft voice.

"What for? If you don't mind me asking?"

"Arson," she says, eyes on her plate.

"Arson?" I try not to repeat the word too loud. "Really?"

"Yep. But she's reformed." Ava raises her head to meet my eyes. "Jessica's worked really hard in her therapy sessions. She's come so far. I'm really proud of her. She's actually due to get out soon."

"Wow," I say again.

"I don't blame her for the crimes she committed," Ava continues. "Not anymore. Jessica always bottled things up instead of talking about them. It's what led to the fires."

"Bottling things up?"

"It was her release. An exit for everything bad we lived through." A far-away look came to her eyes. A sad look. "She told me that, when she was standing and watching the flames she'd lit, it was like…like a cleansing."

We sit quietly for a few moments. All I hear is the call of the gulls over the cabin.

"And what about you?" I finally say. "What was your release?"

She looks up at me and smiles. "Music."

Later that night, as I lie on the couch, wide-awake and staring at the dark ceiling, I think about Ava and Jessica. I think about how awful their childhood must have been. Mine wasn't great, but at least it wasn't like that. It's hard to believe that anyone could come out of that unscathed.

But no matter how hard I look, all I can see is beauty. Not a single flaw.

* * *

I wake to the faint sound of conversation coming through the closed door of my room. I strain to hear. All I can make out are a few words: *price, labour, transmission.* I quietly get off the couch and tiptoe to the washroom. I want to freshen up so she doesn't come out of the bedroom and see my scary morning face.

By the time she comes out of the room, I'm just finishing making coffee.

"Good morning," I say, pouring her a cup. "How did you sleep?"

She tells me how comfortable the bed is, how she was out cold as soon as she lay down. "How was the couch?"

"It's great," I lie, not wanting her to feel guilty.

With me off work and Ava waiting on her car, we have the day ahead of us. I suggest we find something fun to do. It's been a long time since I've been on the Island, so I'm at a loss on what interesting things there are to do here now.

"Maybe if we just get in the car and drive, something will come to us," I say. "But before we take off, I've got to look in on my father."

"Can I come with?"

I imagine Ava meeting my dad. "Oh. That's really sweet of you to offer, but I don't think it's a good idea."

"I'm not the type of friend he'd approve of?"

"No. I mean, of course you are. It's not that. It's just...he's not your typical parental figure. He's more of the dad from hell."

Ava laughs. "Oh, come on. He can't be that bad."

"Tell that to the half-dozen care-aids that won't be returning to his house. Hence the reason I'm here."

She gives me a level look "Mila, he's going to see me around here eventually. Isn't it best that you're up front about who your houseguest is?"

I pause for a moment, half-thinking about how I can talk her out of coming next door, and half-considering what she said.

I look into her eyes. If she's going to meet my dad, I need to make sure she understands what she'll be walking into.

"Ava, it's very sweet that you want to meet him, but you need to grasp the gravity of the situation before we go over there."

Ava gives me a disbelieving smile.

"Did you ever see the movie about the Grinch?"

"Of course, didn't every child?"

"Well, my dad is kind of like that, except piss-drunk."

Ava giggles. "Now you've piqued my curiosity. I'm going to have a quick shower and get ready, then we'll go, ok?"

Ava cheerfully skips into the bedroom briefly, then reappears carrying a change of clothes, shampoo, and make-up bag. As soon as she's in the bathroom, I throw my arms up in defeat and wonder how badly her meeting my father is going to screw up the rest of our day.

I slip into my room and grab a form-fitting Henley and a pair of jeans from my closet. As I quickly change into my clothes, I listen to the shower run and obsess about my dad's reaction when he meets Ava.

Maybe he won't be so bad, I tell myself.

Fifteen minutes later, we're walking into Dad's cabin. And as predicted, he lives up to his reputation and behaves like the king of all assholes.

"Who's the tart?" is all he says to Ava. He cuts off my explanation by berating me for being stupid enough to have a stranger stay at my cabin.

I turn and guide Ava out of the cabin, shutting the door on my father's rant.

I face her, not sure what to say. Ava shrugs and smiles at me, having apparently taken the unpleasant interlude on the chin. "Let it go," she tells me softly as we walk to my car.

I don't know how she can be so resilient. The anger I feel could power a train.

How dare that man verbally attack such a sweet girl? What kind of monster would intentionally try to hurt someone they don't even know?

* * *

Just past the *Welcome to Nanaimo* sign, Ava points to a blue banner hanging from a tall fence along the highway.

"Bungee Jumping!" she says excitedly. "I've always wanted to try it!"

I smile nervously, suddenly forgetting the anger I'm feeling toward Dad. "Really? You've never been?"

"No way. I've never had anyone to go with me." She elbows me. "Until now."

Shit. How the hell am I going to get out of this one? "I didn't catch the name of the place," I say, trying to sound indifferent. "So I don't—"

"I saw it, don't worry. I'm going to call."

Much to my horror, she pulls her phone out of her purse to look up the company.

"Are you sure you want to do this?" I ask, still keeping up the nonchalant facade.

"Hell yeah! Don't you?"

"Well, I've done it before."

"That's so awesome."

"I dunno…the thrill might be gone, doing it again."

"No way! It'll be even more fun because I'm with you."

She calls the number and presses the phone to her ear, beaming at me.

My heart rate accelerates and my hands start to sweat. Maybe I should yank the steering wheel and pull over. I could tell her something is wrong with my car. *No, she'll smell a rat for sure.*

I could claim to have cramps, and even though I'd love to jump with her, I don't think my stomach would hold up. *No, that won't work, either. If I had something wrong with my guts, I would've mentioned it sooner.*

I'm screwed. I can't think of any excuse that won't make me look like a chicken shit.

What's worse is that I'd panicked and lied to her about bungee jumping previously. I've never even considered it. Now, I'll not only have to plummet off a bridge to what could be my death, but I'll have to pretend I'm unfazed by it because she thinks I've done it before.

Ava ends the call. "They're not busy, so we can go straight there!" she squeals. "It's easy to get there, too. We just take the next exit, cross the highway and…"

My heart knocks on the inside of my chest and my head spins. Ava's voice fades and starts to sound like she's talking under water.

"Mila?" Her sudden concerned tone snaps me to attention. "Are you ok? You're looking a little pale."

"Yeah, I'm great. Why?"

She stares at me for a couple of beats, then resumes her excitement. "I can't believe we're actually doing this. It's going to be great!"

I force a smile. "Yeah, neat."

"You'll have to walk me through it, since you've done it before."

Oh good! Not only will I be using all of my muscles in trying not to piss myself, but I'll have to simultaneously act like I know the drill.

I've been thrust into a tornado. The only way out is by challenging my mortality and sailing off a bridge headfirst.

Ava reminds me where to turn once I'm across the highway. I barely park before she's jumping out, bouncing with excitement.

I shake my head. I've never seen anybody this excited to die before.

Hold it together Mila. If you're going to plunge to your death, do it with bravery. Or do your best to fake it.

I lock the car and walk slowly behind her, smiling whenever she looks back at me. Then, through the trees, the metal stairway appears. The entrance to my demise.

I grab onto the railing and with each step, I feel my weakening knees knock. This is the worst thing I've ever done. Why couldn't Ava have seen a sign for a petting zoo? Now that's an adventure I'd be more than happy to participate in.

We reach the top of the stairs and stand at the beginning of a narrow, grated bridge that spans over a river below. We are so high up, I can look down and see the tops of the Giant Douglas Firs.

There's a building to the right with a sign that says *Office*. "Come on," Ava says, grabbing my hand. "This is going to be great!"

A girl about nineteen is standing behind the window. She slides two forms through the open slot and asks us to fill them out. I'm so terror-stricken, I'm not sure if I'm putting the correct information in the right spots. When we're finished with the forms, Ava pays and tells me it's her treat. I don't argue. Why would I fight to pay when it was her idea to put me through this torture?

Two guys in their thirties walk out of the office and motion for us to follow them. I try not to look down—my bones are Jell-O as we make our way over the narrow bridge. Ava looks like a kid seeing Disneyland for the first time. Holding her hand, I can feel the raw excitement coursing through her body. She can probably feel the same level of energy coming off me, except mine is less excitement and more a sheer terror vibe. I feel so chicken right now, I wouldn't be surprised if feathers started sprouting from my ass.

The first thing they do is strap us into harnesses, then Velcro strap the bungee around our ankles. Velcro? Really? I don't want the last thing I hear to be the sound of Velcro ripping apart. When they wrap thick straps overtop of the Velcro, I feel a tiny bit better.

Next, they tell Ava and I to stand facing one another. I suddenly remember last night, thinking about how I couldn't find a flaw in her. I look into those beautiful green eyes and all I can think is, *What the hell is wrong with her head to want this?*

She's smiling—glowing, in fact. "I'm stoked that you're here with me. I'm so freaked out I could scream."

I briefly look down and see rocks on either side of the river. My mind flashes to a Road Runner cartoon where Wile E. Coyote strapped himself to a rocket and ended up ass over teakettle, his body half-buried in the ground and ass sticking up in the air. Today I am Wile E. Coyote, only I'm strapped to a reckless blonde instead of a rocket.

The two men help us shuffle to the edge of the platform. Then they tell us to hug each other tightly.

No shit, Einstein. As soon as we're falling, I'll be holding onto her so tight that her ribs will pop out her neck.

As I press my body against Ava's, I feel her heart pounding, or maybe it's mine. One of the men has a hold of us while the other guy counts. "3...2...1..."

And just like that, we're hurtling toward the water below. My stomach flips, and I can only stare at the river getting larger and larger as we drop.

Suddenly, we reach the end of the cord, and we spring back up toward the underside of the bridge. Ava's deafening screams of exhilaration echo off the water and rocks around us.

We bounce a few more times before beginning our slow, upside-down ascent back to the platform.

"This was the best!" Ava says, before looking into my face. "Oh wow. You look like you're going to be sick. Are you ok?"

"Perfect," I grunt. "I'm just trying to find my stomach."

Ava giggles. "You'll feel better once you're right-side-up."

Once back on the bridge, we get untied, thank the crew, then head toward the car. It's only once we reach the gravel parking lot when I notice Ava's been holding my hand the entire time.

"Wasn't that a blast?" She gives my hand a squeeze. "We did something neither one of us have ever done before. That was a bonding experience!"

I blink at her. "How did you know I hadn't done it before?"

"Oh, come on," she giggles. "You were horrified."

My face feels hot, but I laugh. "When did you guess that it was my first time?"

"Right around the time I said the words *bungee jump* and all of the blood drained from your face. But don't you feel better for going through with it?"

"I feel better that I lived through it, if that's what you're asking."

She laughs, then leans over and wraps her arms around my neck. "I'm so glad I met you."

"Same here, but next time, I get to pick the adventure."

She snickers and nods.

After having a nice fish and chips meal in Nanaimo, we head home. It's during this trip when Ava brings up my mom. She first asks how my parents met, then later how Mom died, and if her passing was the reason I moved off the Island.

"I was still living at home when Mom got the call from the doctor," I say softly. "The call saying that the biopsy from a lump on her chest was malignant. By the time we swallowed the news, a follow-up appointment with the specialist hit us with the final blow—the cancer had spread and there was no hope for recovery. From then on everything in our lives seemed to deteriorate along with Mom.

"Within six months, I was caring for both of my parents full time. At the same time I was trying to complete my education to become a teacher, a goal that I'd never reach. My mom would've been disappointed to learn that, especially since I ended up doing something she would've felt was beneath me—working as a nanny for a lawyer and his wife. And yeah, it definitely wasn't my dream job, but it got me off the Island and away from the verbal punching matches my dad and I would get into."

She reaches over and rubs my shoulder. "I don't think you should judge yourself by what you do for a living. It doesn't define you as a human being. Your character does."

I smile and nod. "You know, you're a pretty bright girl…for a blonde."

"Oh really? For a blonde?"

I glance at her and smile.

Chapter Six

It's hard to believe that just a couple of months ago, I was dreading being back in Ladysmith to care for my cantankerous father. I thought I would be miserable and struggling with our residual issues. It's not like he's been easy. But if I hadn't come, I would never have met Ava.

In my past relationships, I've always felt like I was teetering on the edge of a rockface, gazing below at broken stones of past heartbreaks. With Ava, the direction of my focus is forever changed. I am no longer looking down. Now I find myself looking ahead, at the future.

After her car was repaired, Ava decided that she didn't want to drive off and resume the life of playing music up and down the Island. Instead, she cancelled her upcoming gigs and opted to stay at the cabin with me. Not long after that, I moved from the couch to the bedroom. We spend our days laughing, growing closer, and making love.

Sometimes, when we're lying in bed and I wake before she does, I look over at her perfect face and watch her sleep. I still can't believe how lucky I am that this beautiful creature walked into my life.

My father still doesn't like her, but then again, he doesn't like anyone. At least he's become more tolerant, letting her pick up laundry or drop off the odd grocery item.

His health is slowly declining. The one positive thing is that he's stopped drinking in the daytime and only dips into the bottle after dinner.

* * *

Ava wakes me up with a cup of coffee and toast. We don't have a platter, so the items are put beside me on top of a pizza pan. I rub my eyes and look up at her. The morning sun glows behind her, illuminating her golden hair.

"Good morning, beautiful," I say, looking down at the pizza pan. "What did I do to deserve breakfast in bed?"

"Nothing. I just wanted you to start your day off right."

She leans down and presses her soft lips against mine before sliding in beside me.

As soon as I've had a sip of coffee and a bite of toast, Ava says, "I have some news."

"Good news or bad news?" I put my cup down. "Is it about upcoming gigs that'll take you away from me? Because that would be bad news."

"No. It's nothing like that. I just found out that my sister Jessica is being released tomorrow. I have to go to Victoria to pick her up."

"Oh. Wow. Ok. Where are you dropping her off?"

"Well, I kind of wanted to talk to you about that."

There's a sinking feeling in my gut and I set down the piece of toast.

"Jess has to have a contact and an address when she gets out." Ava picks at the bedsheet, not looking at me. "I know this place is tiny, and it just suits our needs, but I was wondering how you'd feel about Jess staying with us for a short time until she can tie down her own place. What do you think?"

I say nothing for a few seconds. I'm not one to judge another person, but something tells me that after a person's been in jail, they're left with even more issues—reintegrating isn't an immediate thing.

Then, of course, there's the whole arson thing. And the fact that we live in a wood cabin.

Everything about this makes me feel uneasy. But if I say no, Ava will be upset, maybe even resentful. We've become so close in such a short period of time—I don't want to risk ruining that.

"She'd be staying here only until she can find her own place?"

Ava nods. "Yes. And I promise it won't take long because I'll be helping her."

I take her hand. "Ok. It's alright with me if it's what you want."

"It is. I miss her terribly." She wraps her arms around my neck and kisses my cheek. "Thank you."

Ava goes to have a quick shower while I finish my breakfast. "I might go to the beach today," she calls over the running faucet.

I slip out of bed and discard my mostly uneaten toast, then sit on the couch to wait for the shower to be free.

I look up at the picture of my mom hanging on the wall. I wonder if she'd be happy with how I'm caring for Dad. I wonder if she'd like Ava.

She probably wouldn't think I was doing enough for my father. Deep down, I know I could be doing a better job. Regardless of him being an unmanageable jerk, I should spend more time cleaning his place and overseeing his meds. With Ava's sister coming, the girls will be getting reacquainted and I should have more time to spend at Dad's. So maybe it's a good thing.

A waft of steam escapes through the bathroom door when Ava walks out with a towel on her head. With only an hour until my shift starts, I dart into the bathroom.

As I get undressed, I notice a pill bottle on the side of the sink. I pick it up and read the label. *Ava Fellows*, and at the bottom of the label, the word *Olanzapine*.

She's never mentioned anything about taking pills. I wonder what she takes them for. I want to ask her, but something tells me not to. If she hasn't mentioned it in the time we've been together, she's either not comfortable telling me or embarrassed about why she needs them. Maybe it's best that I wait until she brings it up.

Nevertheless, I leave the cabin preoccupied, my mind whirling with the upcoming visit and how it might affect the bond I have with Ava.

* * *

The next morning, angry dark clouds roll overhead as the sea churns and tosses white foam onto the shore. Ava left an hour ago for Victoria to pick up Jessica. All morning my stomach has been in knots. To take my mind off the visit, I head next door to check on Dad.

He looks like he's lost weight. His head is large compared to his body—it makes me think of an orange on a toothpick. I feel guilty when I see the dirty floor and the dust on the window ledges. The past few months, I've spent most of my time focussing on my new relationship.

I promise myself to do better. Regardless of the volatile relationship I have with my father, the initial reason I came here was to care for him.

I spend the rest of the morning on the floors, the bathroom and the dusting while he grumbles at the TV.

After I finish dusting the last windowsill, I sit down at the table with a glass of water. "Dad?"

"What? Can't you see I'm watching TV?"

"I can see you arguing with the TV. And, not to burst your bubble, but I'm pretty sure your efforts are futile. The people on the screen can't hear you, and even if they could, they'd probably think you were a lunatic."

Much to my surprise, he doesn't holler at me. Instead, he starts to laugh.

"Dad," I say, glancing at the window. "When's the last time you got out of this place?"

"I don't know," he says, straining to remember. "Since before you came. My meals and meds are delivered and the doctor pops by once a month, so, yeah, it's been a while."

I stand. "It's unhealthy for you to stay cooped up in here. Why don't you get dressed and I'll take you for a car ride? We'll drive to town, I'll get us take-out, and we can park by the water and eat?"

"That's the stupidest damn idea ever. Sounds like a lot of effort to me. If I want to see the water, all I have to do is look out the window."

"Why does everything have to be a fight with you? You're always bitching about the quality of the meals that are delivered, so let's go and get you something better."

He hums and haws for a while, then finally grumbles, "I guess I don't really have much choice. If I don't come, you'll never shut up about it."

I smile. "Bingo!"

Dad slowly gets up from the couch, then maneuvers into his wheelchair and heads for his room to get changed.

Once he's out of sight, I holler, "Do you need any help getting dressed?"

"Have you lost your mind?" he immediately yells back.

I chuckle.

After completing the laborious task of getting my father into the passenger seat, I fold the wheelchair up and lean it against the cabin. Once in the car, I buckle up and look over at Dad. "Doing ok?"

His brow furrows. "What the hell kind of question is that? Of course I'm doing ok. I'm not a child. Save your nanny skills for that imp you take care of in Vancouver."

"Imp? Really?" I shake my head. "You know, I'm pretty sure you'd never make it as a mall Santa."

"Sure I would. I wouldn't cause the kids any harm. If a kid was bad, I'd just slap the parent."

"Yeah, that would make you popular, alright."

I turn on the stereo and Arlo Guthrie's "Alice's Restaurant" comes on. Right away, I can see my father's mood lighten. Listening to the song and looking out the window at the beautiful trees and foliage, his posture changes from rigid to relaxed. When Arlo breaks into the chorus, I notice him tapping his boney fingers in time with the music. Though, the biggest change is the sudden lack of bitching and swearing.

I drive slowly to town so he can take in the sights. Thankfully, the traffic in town isn't too busy, and we're able to leisurely look for somewhere appealing to eat.

Dad opts for fish and chips, something we ate a lot when I was young. I put the newspaper-wrapped meals in the backseat and drive to a stretch of road that faces the beach.

I grab one of the packets, open the folded newspaper and place the food on his lap. Then I squeeze a ketchup pack on his chips and take the lid off the tartar sauce for him. Staring at the food with disapproval, he announces how I've done it all wrong.

Ignoring his bullshit, I eat my meal while looking out at the whitecaps dancing on the turbulent, grey sea.

After we're finished our meal, I crumple up the newspapers and toss them in the back before looking over at Dad. "So, what should we do next?"

"How the hell should I know? This whole outing was your idea."

"Does that mean I get to take you anywhere I want?"

"I don't care."

"That's good, because I've got a great idea. I think it'd be a really good experience for you to try something new. It'll probably give you a whole new outlook on life."

He looks perplexed as he stares out the window. "You better tell me what you're thinking of doing, in case I think it's stupid."

"Oh come on, Dad. Do you really want me to ruin the surprise? Where's your sense of adventure?"

I start the car and he continues to look out the window. "Tell me what you're up to!"

I try my hardest not to snicker. "Ok. Ok. Don't get your shorts in a knot. I'm taking you…bungee jumping!"

With this, his head snaps around. "Have you lost your damn mind?"

I grin. "What? What's the matter with bungee jumping? It's so much fun—it's like you're a human yo-yo. And it's great for your bones. Any back pain you have immediately goes away when the bungee yanks your body to an abrupt halt."

"Yeah, I bet it'd be good for my digestive tract too, right after I shit myself."

We bust out in simultaneous laughter. I pull out of the parking spot. "Do you want me to stop for anything on the way home?"

"Nah. I'm good." Dad fumbles with the stereo until he finds a Dylan song. He turns up the volume and leans back in the seat.

I don't say anything during the drive. Instead, I replay the sound of his laughter in my mind, wondering how many years it's been since I last heard him laugh like that.

After we pull up to the cabin, I get out to retrieve the wheelchair. He yells at me and tells me that he doesn't need it, and with the minimal help of my arm, he carefully walks to the door.

By the time he's sitting on the couch and has gotten his shoes off, he's out of breath and exhausted. I grab his pillow from the bedroom along with a throw blanket and put them beside him.

I check the time. It's already 4PM and Ava and her sister should be showing up soon. I get Dad a glass of water and make sure he has everything he needs before walking next door to my place, where I do a few last-minute fixups around the living room so it looks tidy. Then I sit on the couch and wait.

* * *

It's 10PM when I hear Ava's car pull up.

I've had a power nap and read part of a Tom Clancy novel to pass the time. I quickly jump up and finger comb my hair before walking out of the bedroom.

The front door opens and Ava walks in, carrying a canvas pack.

She smiles at me apologetically. "Sorry we're so late. Jessica had to stop at a friend's place to grab some clothing."

She drops the bag on the floor and gives me a hug, just as her sister comes through the door.

She's around the same height as Ava, the same build too. Lanky and fit. However, from the neck up, they are polar opposites. Jessica has long, raven hair and striking crystal blue eyes. But, like her sister, she's breathtakingly beautiful.

"Hi, Jessica," I say. "It's nice to meet you."

Her eyes briefly meet mine as she packs in a small suitcase and drops it on the sofa. "Wow man, this place is micro-small." She thunders her way through the cabin, opening the bathroom door. "Wow, look how small your john is.".

Ava looks at me, half-smiling, and shrugs.

* * *

After Jessica's things are put away, they decide to order pizza. I retire to the bedroom and give them the living room to talk and get caught up.

Not to mention that something about Jessica rubs me the wrong way, and I'd rather not be in the same room with her if I can avoid it.

Jessica's loud voice cuts through the wall. She's telling Ava about the politics of prison life. I wish I had earplugs when she relives incidents of violence between the inmates and the guards. As if Ava needs to hear all that crap. I hope she doesn't think Jessica's crazy stories are exciting or cool.

It's late when Ava finally crawls into bed beside me. I can tell she's tired by the way her head hits the pillow. I roll over and look into her eyes. "Are you happy to see your sister?"

"I am," she says with a smile. "But I feel so badly for her. Some of the things she told me are shocking. The inmates are treated like animals."

Like criminals, you mean, I feel like saying, but I don't. Instead, she rolls over and I snuggle against her.

* * *

It's day two of the Jessica Experience.

As we get dressed, I want to ask Ava what their plans are for the day, and if, perhaps, they'll be apartment hunting for Jessica, but I don't want her to think I'm being pushy.

In the kitchen, I see Jessica standing over the sink with a bag of coffee in one hand and my Bodum press in the other.

"I can show you how to use that, if you like." I hold out my hand.

She glances at me. "Why the hell do you have this confusing thing?"

I take the coffee and the press and set them down on the counter before plugging in the kettle. "It'll just be a minute."

As I pour the coffee in the press, Jessica walks over to the window and looks out at the calm water. "You guys are in the middle of nowhere here, huh?"

"I don't know. I never thought of it that way. I like the peacefulness of living outside town."

She scoffs. "Yeah, I'd go nuts living out here with nothing to do."

I'm glad you feel that way, I say to myself. "So, Jessica, what have you and Ava got planned for today?"

"Trying to get rid of me already, huh? You want me to find a place, huh?"

"What?" I shake my head. "Of course not!"

I finish making coffee and pour her a cup. She walks up beside me and shakes the sugar bowl over her coffee, scattering the sticky granules all over the counter.

"Oops," she says, before opening the fridge to grab the milk and closing the door with a kick. I'm trying to hide my disapproving expression as she carries her cup to the couch, spilling coffee on the floor and wiping the spots up with her socked foot.

Usually I hate leaving for my shift, wanting instead to stay home with Ava. Today, I can't wait to get out of here.

Ava walks out of the bedroom and puts her arms around my neck. "I meant to ask— how was the time with your dad yesterday?"

I pour her a coffee as I begin to tell her about taking Dad for a car ride and lunch. Then, suddenly, Jessica interrupts: "Hey, sis. I'll need a ride into town. I've got to touch base with my probation officer."

Immediately, Ava's attention turns to Jessica. I finish fixing the coffee and hand it to Ava, who is completely absorbed in her sister's endless chatter. I go into the bedroom and bide my time until I can leave.

* * *

An unsettled wind gusts up the streets, sending leaves and debris swirling through the air. Most weather is fine to deal with while I'm in the car, but if I pick up a fare with groceries, I've got to get out and help with the bags as dust and leaves blow into my face.

Still, I like my job. The locals are always friendly and talkative. Though, lately, there has been a shift in the normal topics of conversation.

Instead of discussing the weather or current attractions, now the line of conversation immediately goes to the growing issue of drug houses springing up in the community. More often than not, this is immediately followed by sharp words on how the cops aren't doing their jobs. I've learned my lesson—instead of defending the police again, I nod and smile and take them where they want to go.

Back at the office, Don talks about how there's apparently five or six suspected rental homes in town where drugs are being either made or dealt. "It's a bad situation," he says, shaking his head. "Most of the criminals aren't even from here. They come from the mainland or bigger cities on the Island. No wonder we're seeing more overdoses and fights and break-ins. The pubs and the nightclub had to hire more security at night. People are afraid to go out in the evenings. It's a damn shame. It's changing the whole easy, laid-back vibe that Ladysmith has always been known for."

He's right. In Vancouver, drugs and other crimes are always a factor, but there are still safe neighborhoods. Ladysmith is so small that one bad area affects the whole town.

Chapter Seven

It's been two weeks since Jessica has graced us with her presence.

I work, come home, eat, then retire to the bedroom to read until Ava comes to bed. It's not uncommon for me to wade over Jessica's clothes, purses and other crap when I get up in the morning, and her loud voice grates on my ears every hour of the day.

I've yet to bring up Jessica moving out. I don't want to put Ava under pressure. But my patience for Jessica is wearing thin.

I can't escape to work today, so instead I'll spend some time with Dad before having to return to the cabin. Usually I'd spend the rest of the day in my room, but the girls have been planning on having a fire in the pit on the beach tonight. Ava bought hotdogs and marshmallows and she's already packed up the lawn chairs.

I'm sure Ava invited me along because she wants to include me, but I'm sure my invitation also has something to do with Jessica being a known arsonist, and if the cops showed up it'd probably look better if the two sisters weren't the only ones lighting a fire.

* * *

The wind is mellow and the sea is calm. Light waves creep up the shore, creating fluffy layers of white foam that glow under the night sky.

Ava and I sit on one side of the fire while Jessica sits across from us. As I stoke the fire with small pieces of kindling, I look up at Jessica's face and the orange light of the flames on her pale skin. Her raven hair and piercing blue eyes look almost evil as she stares into the center of the blaze, like a witch from a child's storybook.

Ava pushes wieners on thin rods while I pour ginger ale into plastic cups. Jessica fixes the hotdog buns. For a few minutes things are almost pleasant. That is, until Jessica starts with jailhouse anecdotes about fights, sex and the seedy politics that go on behind bars.

Time drags on as I'm forced to listen. In the cabin, I can hide in the bedroom, but here I've got no escape.

Finally, Ava senses my disinterest in Jessica's jailhouse tales and changes the subject. "I have a gig in a week," she says. "At the Joker Lounge."

Jessica seems put out by the news. "I'd love to go with you, but my probation officer wouldn't allow it."

As the girls talk, something occurs to me. If Ava is away and Jessica can't go with her, does that mean she'll be at the cabin with me, alone? Just the two of us?

Immediately I lose my appetite and discard the rest of my hotdog.

For the next hour, I watch as Jessica pics up sticks and debris from the beach and throws them into the fire. When she finds pieces of an old rocker, I stop her before she has time to toss them in the pit. Thankfully Ava gets cold, and we have a good excuse to go home.

That night, as usual, Ava and I go to sleep immediately after the light is off. The moment Jessica walked into our lives, any love-making—or any intimacy at all— between Ava and I vanished. I miss the warm feeling of her kiss on my body, the openness and playfulness we've always shared. By the time I'm home from work and Ava is finished catering to Jessica's insatiable need for attention, there's no energy left over for us.

* * *

Another week has passed and as far as I know, no progress has been made with finding Jessica a place to live.

Ava walks into the front room, carrying a small bag and her guitar case. I'm making a quick sandwich to take to work and Jessica is sitting on the couch, surrounded by boxes of half-eaten snacks.

I point at Ava with my butter knife. "Are you running away from home?"

Ava smiles. "I'm just putting my things in the car so I'm ready for work tonight."

"I've been thinking," Jessica pipes up. "I don't think there's any danger in me coming to watch you play."

I feel a bubble of hope, which is immediately popped when Ava shakes her head. "You, sweet sister, have a curfew. You don't want to do anything to screw up your probation."

Jessica nods and starts digging through her purse.

Once I've packed my sandwich and an apple into my bag, I walk up to Ava and kiss her on the cheek. "I'll be home around 8PM, so if you've left for work, call me when you're on a break."

Ava is just about to answer me when Jessica hollers, "Yes! I found it." She's holding a small brown address book in her hand. "I have a friend or two that used to live in this puddle jumper town. I wonder if they're still here?"

Ava looks at me and smiles. "Have a good day."

* * *

My shift goes by with relative ease. Most of the fares are older folks coming and going from the bingo hall, the grocery store, and the local pubs. I find out from Don at the end of my shift that today is Seniors Day, which makes sense when I count the paltry amount of tips in my pocket.

On the way home, I purposefully pass by The Joker Lounge. I want to stop in and watch Ava play, but this is the first time she's had time away from both me and Jessica. I don't want her to feel suffocated. Instead, I turn up the tunes and drive back to the cabin.

I didn't have enough time this morning to check on Dad. Even though it's just after eight, and he's probably well into his whiskey, I should at least make an appearance and make sure he has everything he needs.

As soon as I near his door, I can hear him hollering and griping about something. I knock until he opens the door.

"Hurry up and get in here," he says. "You're letting all the damn bugs in."

Dad wheels in front of the TV, then hops out of his chair onto the couch. I scan the area where he's sitting and look for the bottle. I can't see one, not even on the counters or on the table.

He sees me scoping. "What the hell you lookin' for?" he grumbles.

He's not drunk. His voice, although gruff and abrupt, is clear and lacks the usual slur I've come to expect this time of night.

Just as I sit down on the sofa, he points at the screen. "Look at that asshole. Condescending fool. I'd kick his ass if he was in front of me."

I look at the screen. "Dad. That's Alex Trebek. He's not trying to be condescending, he's just enunciating so the contestants understand the questions."

"Don't care. He's an asshole."

I laugh. "It literally wouldn't matter who you were watching—to you, they're all assholes. You and Mom used to watch Jeopardy when I was a kid. I never remember you attacking him before."

"That's because I didn't want your mother to know that I was onto her."

"What are you talking about?"

"She had the hots for him."

"What? For Alex Trebek?"

"That's right!" he says, glaring at the TV.

"Why in the heck would you ever think that?"

"Because once, when we were watching the show, your mother made some comment about Alex Trebek being a Canadian. Why the hell would she know that unless she did some digging on him?"

"Dad. I hate to break it to you, but everyone knows he was Canadian. It's common knowledge. They probably mentioned it during one of the broadcasts. You're being ridiculous."

"She also said he had nice hair! What do you think now, smartass?"

"I think you're nuttier than squirrel poo."

Dad shakes his head and chuckles.

I sit with him for the next half hour until his program ends. When I get him a glass of water and a bag of chips, I look up at the clock. I've only been here for an hour.

Wanting to waste as much time as possible, I opt to organize Dad's cupboards and shelves. Dad changes the channel to a Green Acres rerun and within five minutes, I hear him chattering about the size of Eva Gabor's boobs. If my mother was here, she'd be rolling her eyes and shaking her head.

After cleaning and dusting, I decide it's time to wander next door. At least I'll only have to put up with the house crasher for another hour before Ava gets home.

As soon as I open the door to the cabin, I feel the absence of energy.

I do a quick look through the rooms and see that I'm alone. Jessica isn't here.

I breathe a sigh of relief just as my cell rings. It's Ava. I hear the chatter of people in the background at the lounge as Ava asks me how my day was. She has one more set to do before she heads home.

"I'm looking forward to seeing you," I say, glancing around at the empty cabin. For once, we can hang out without Jessica lurking nearby.

"Hey," Ava says suddenly, "can you let Jessica know that her cell is dead? I've been trying to text her all evening and she hasn't answered me."

"Sure. I mean, I would, but she's not here."

Instantly, there's panic in Ava's voice. "What do you mean she's not there? I dropped her off at a pizza place in town at 6:45. She told me she was meeting an old friend and was getting dropped off at the cabin. Did you check the bedroom? Maybe she crashed on our bed."

"It's a small place, sweetie. If she were a fly, I would've seen her by now."

"It's been hours. She promised that she'd behave herself and stick to her curfew. And here she is, pulling a disappearing act. I can't believe it."

I feel sorry for Ava. I can tell how much she loves Jessica and how badly she wants her sister to get on the right path. I want to ease her nerves, especially since she still has another set to do. "I bet she'll walk through the door any minute. Try not to focus on it. Just have a good set and come home. I'm sure everything will be fine."

Ava sighs. "I guess there's not much else I can do."

After we hang up, I sit on the sofa and look out the window into the dark night.

When Ava wanted Jessica to stay here, I had a bad feeling it was going to cause Ava and me a lot of stress. As predicted, it's starting.

* * *

I'm half asleep on the couch when Ava gets home. Her face looks ashen and drawn, weighed down by Jessica's absence.

I stand up and walk over to her. "Don't worry, ok? You can't control what your sister does or doesn't do. You're a damn good sister to her and no matter what happens, you need to remember that."

"Thanks," she says, looking down at the floor. "I think I'm going to have a shower."

Tension fills the small cabin until the air is so heavy, I feel like I'm suffocating. Ava paces back and forth, only stopping long enough to check her phone for messages. My best attempts at distracting her fail. Every question or subject matter I raise is answered with short responses, just enough to shut me up.

Out of options, and feeling invisible, I decide that my presence is neither helping nor preventing Ava from worrying about Jessica. I gently excuse myself and go to bed.

* * *

At first the voices are faint. Then they grow louder, both angry, both escalating until I'm fully awake and sitting up.

I look at Ava's side of the bed and notice the blanket hasn't been touched. I check the time: it's just after three in the morning. I slip out of bed and grab my housecoat on the way out of the room.

Jessica is standing by the front door. Her arms are crossed and she looks blitzed on something. Ava is facing her, hands on her hips. Both girl's voices have now escalated to a full yell, neither listening to the other.

"Is everything ok here?" I ask, putting my housecoat on.

"Mind your own business, Mila," hollers Jessica.

"Don't speak to her that way," Ava yells. "It's because of her you have a place to stay."

"Are you serious? You're yelling at me and defending her? You don't even know her. Where's your loyalty to your own flesh and blood?"

Ava turns to me. "Mila, can I just talk to her alone right now?"

Back in my room, I sit on the edge of the bed and listen to the heated debate through the door, hoping like hell Ava tells her sister to leave.

Inaudible words get lost between the two rooms with only the odd yell clear enough to penetrate through the wood. After about twenty minutes Ava walks into the bedroom, slamming the door behind her. She looks winded and her face is red with frustration. "I'm so sorry about that," she says.

"Don't worry about it. Did you two work it out?"

"I guess so. She's going to bed now, hopefully she'll sleep off whatever drugs are in her system."

"I'm sorry you have to deal with this. I know how much you want her to do well."

Ava walks over and sits next to me. "I can handle just about anything she does, except this. I just can't believe she's chosen to get stoned when she knows how drugs devastated our family. If she thinks I'm just going to sit idly by and let her destroy her life by becoming a dope head, she's sadly mistaken."

I place my arm around her. "I know you love your sister," I say gently. "I know you want the best for her. But ultimately it's her choice to sort herself out. It's not on you."

Ava's body stiffens and she shifts away from me. "No. That's not how I see it. If Jess wants to go down the same path that my parents did, she'll meet huge opposition from me. There's no way I'm going to sit back and watch as she kills herself."

I move closer to bridge the gap she created. "All you can do is live by example. And the most important thing is to set healthy boundaries for yourself. Maybe she'll be influenced by you and follow suit."

"It's not as easy as that. Look at your father. Don't tell me that you're ok with his incessant drinking."

I take a deep breath before I respond. "I didn't say that you should be unaffected by the bad decisions Jessica makes. I never said that my father's drinking doesn't affect me. I just don't want you to feel like Jessica's failures are a reflection of you not doing enough."

Ava fidgets with her hand. For a moment we sit in silence, until she suddenly gets up. "It's late. I think we both need to get some sleep." She walks to the other side of the bed and crawls in.

With her back to me and mine to her, I barely get any rest. It's only with the first flashes of the sun rising that my brain slows enough to sleep.

* * *

Both girls are still asleep when I quietly slip out of the cabin.

I don't have to work until this evening, but the heavy energy between Jessica and Ava is making me feel too weighed down. When the cabin door is closed behind me, I stand on the steps and draw in a deep breath of fresh air.

Needing a coffee to perk me up, I head into town. With each mile between me and the cabin, the lighter I feel.

The early sun casts a pinkish glow over the town, bringing with it the few early risers getting a walk in while the day is still young and quiet. I drive up and down the sleepy streets, looking for an open sign in a café window. Finally, I spot the same little java shop I went to when I first came back to town.

The desirable aroma of freshly brewed coffee wafts out the door as I step inside, where a group of elderly residents are gathered at a table. Their friendly smiles greet me as I pass their table and walk up to the counter.

A kindly woman in her sixties takes my order and engages in idle chit chat while she pours me a coffee and gets me a freshly baked muffin. I pull money from my pocket when a man shouts out from behind me, "I'll get that. Don't take her money."

I turn to see my boss, Don, walking up to the counter. I smile and thank him. "What are you doing up so early?"

"The nightshift guy is going home in twenty minutes and I'll be on dayshift. I just stopped in for a coffee before I start the day."

While Don orders, I sit at a table and take a few quick sips. Just as I'm about to take a bite of my muffin, Don walks up. "I guess it was a pretty exciting night."

Perplexed, I look up at him. "Why? What happened?"

"There was a fire near the Nanaimo River last night."

"You're kidding. Did everyone make it out okay?"

"Yeah, from what I hear, there were no injuries. I guess the house was a crack shack or something. My guess is that someone was stoned and lit the blaze by accident."

"What time did this happen?"

Don shrugs. "It wasn't that late. The bars were still open when I heard the first sirens."

I shake my head. "I guess I'll hear all about it driving cab tonight."

Don leaves with a wave. As I drink my coffee, I overhear the odd word about the fire as the retirees huddle at their table in front of me.

Once I'm finished, I walk to my car, checking my phone for messages from Ava once I'm in the driver's seat. There's nothing. Probably still sleeping after her long night of worrying then fighting with Jessica.

Chapter Eight

The morning light seems to evade Dad's cabin, making it seem lifeless and morose. It takes longer than usual for him to open the door to let me in.

Shuffling in front of me with his cane, he seems weaker and more fragile as he finds his way back to the couch. I sit beside him and try to spark up a conversation, but my efforts fail as he answers with short, breathy sentences.

"Dad, you look like crap. What's going on?"

"Quit trying to micromanage me. You're no doctor."

Then, my eye catches the bottle sticking out of the kitchen trash bin. I look over at my father. He's not drunk. I'd be able to tell by the look on his face. And the room is lacking the pungent, unmistakable stench of whiskey.

A few moments of awkward silence pass. Then he abruptly sits up straight, his face set with determination. "That's it. I'm done. I've had enough of this shit. If I have to die, I'd rather it was cancer that takes me out, not whiskey."

I can barely believe what I'm hearing. If he didn't have that look of sincerity, the same one he gets when he's really set on something, I wouldn't believe him. "What have you done with my father? You must be an imposter."

"Keep your sarcasm to yourself."

"I'm sorry, Dad. I just never thought I'd hear you say that you're done with whiskey."

"I just can't handle feeling this shitty in the morning."

I smile and tell him I'm proud of him, even if I do have some skepticism about his claim.

After making Dad some canned soup and putting his medication, water and saltines within arms reach of the couch, I head next door to my cabin.

* * *

Thankfully, Jessica is still asleep on the couch when I get home. I head to the bedroom, where Ava is just waking up.

The sunlight from the window catches Ava's half-open green eyes and she raises both arms, signalling for me to hug her. As I press my body against hers, I realize just how much I've missed the intimacy between us.

"It feels great to hold you again," she says. "I'm sorry if I've messed our lives up by having my sister here." She pauses. "As much as I love her, I sometimes wish she never came to stay with us."

Finally, her words are echoing what I've been feeling all along.

"Mila." She pulls back and takes my hands, looking me deep in the eyes. "I know we haven't known one another for long, but I want you to know that my first priority is to keep my relationship with you intact."

I squeeze her hands. "That's all I needed to hear."

* * *

Jessica stays asleep throughout the day, giving me and Ava the afternoon to have some quality time together.

When I tell her about my father's claim to quit drinking, she hugs me tight. "Maybe, once he's sober, you and he can fix your relationship."

I smile, knowing that my dad isn't one to muddle through the past. Still, I appreciate Ava's words of encouragement.

The light of day fades quickly and gives way to a dark, starry night by the time I head to work in town. As predicted, all my passengers talk about is the fire. Ladysmith is known for being relatively crime-free, so even though the fire happened fifteen minutes toward Nanaimo, this is unsettling news for the people who live and work here.

Ava texts me when she gets to the lounge. Her message is short but sweet: *I loved our cuddle session today. We'll have to do more of that soon. See you when you get off work.*

My shift seems to fly by. I revel in the fact my father has quit drinking, and also because Ava and I are back on track, regardless of Jessica sharing our space.

It's late when I get home. Ava is sitting at the kitchen table with a bucket of chicken and Jessica is transfixed by her cellphone.

Ava and I talk as we eat, then head to bed and cuddle. I want to make love to her, but considering Jessica is just feet away on the other side of the door, I don't instigate anything. Hopefully, we'll have our intimate time back soon.

The next few days are relatively easy. My dad struggles with detoxing but stays the course. Jessica is her normal, outspoken and sometimes obnoxious self, but it's manageable.

I've got one more night shift, then a couple days off. Ava and I plan on going to Nanaimo tomorrow to have some one-on-one time. We're going for a hike and maybe catching a movie. Thankfully, she hasn't invited Jessica.

* * *

It's not until I'm halfway into my shift that I hear the big news from an elderly male passenger. Another fire has broken out in a small cottage on the Nanaimo River. The old guy doesn't have a lot of details—he only knows that the fire department was called. The news is confirmed when at the end of my shift, Don tells me how he heard the exact same story but couldn't elaborate, as the emergency crews were still on-scene.

When I get home it's late, but Ava is still up and is sitting on the couch. When I don't notice Jessica in the cabin, I realize that there's probably another reason she's still awake. "Is everything alright? Where's your sister?"

"Gone," she says. "And she can stay gone for all I care."

I walk over and set my bag on the table, then take a seat next to her. "What happened?"

"Jess was itching to go out all night. I kept trying to talk some reason into her, but she wouldn't listen. She kept repeating that one of her friends was going to pick her up and they were just going for a quick drive, but I knew she was lying. I knew she just wanted to get high again. She wouldn't listen to me and she wouldn't back down. Eventually, she started a big shouting match, and then she left."

"Why didn't you call me? I could've helped."

"I didn't want to mess up your night. And it wouldn't have made a difference. There's nothing you could've done. She's gone and that's all there is to it."

I put my hand on hers. "It's so unfair that you're having to go through this. I really thought that she learned her lesson. I'm sorry."

Ava gets up, walks to the front door and locks it. "I'm tired. I want to forget all about this night and just go to bed." She looks somber and defeated.

I cuddle her until she falls asleep. For a brief moment, I consider getting up and unlocking the door in case Jessica comes home, but I decide against it. I don't want to defy Ava. I wake a couple of times through the dark hours of the early morning, thinking I hear someone outside, but after waiting a few moments, the sound fades and I drift back to sleep.

* * *

Hard rain mixed with small branches and debris slap the single-paned window of the bedroom. I get up and look outside at the morning storm, then grab my housecoat and set out for the kitchen to make me and Ava a pot of coffee. I'm just finishing with the press when Ava walks out of the bedroom.

She doesn't say much as she sips her coffee. I can tell that she woke up in the same way she went to bed—preoccupied about her sister.

"So, it looks pretty miserable outside," I point out, trying to distract her. "Should we plan our outing for another day?"

"I don't mind the storm. I think we should go. If I stay here, I'll just drive myself crazy thinking about my sister."

* * *

On the way to Nanaimo, Ava tells me that she's been working on a new song "It's about a girl who is bound to her family by loyalty, even though they treat her terribly."

I nod. "I can't wait to hear it."

Despite the weather, our day in Nanaimo is just what we both need. We scope out funky little second-hand clothing stores, trying on funny hats and making each other laugh. Then we go to a farmers' market not far from the ferry terminal and buy fresh local produce and organic chicken for me to make for dinner. We listen to tunes and sing along during the drive home, holding hands and stealing the odd kiss.

It's a perfect day... at least, until the last part of our drive home.

On Brenton Page Road, Ava squints through the rapidly swiping windshield wipers at something on the roadside. "Stop," she yells over the music.

I quickly hit the brakes and strain to see what she's looking at. She points, and I see a willowy figure trudging along on the dirt shoulder.

The happiness I've been feeling comes to a screeching halt as we pull up slowly next to the half-drenched Jessica.

Ava rolls down her window and says something to her sister, who promptly opens the back door and jumps in. The girls don't speak the rest of the ride home, and I foresee another verbal boxing match as soon as they get inside and are face-to-face.

After pulling up to the cabin, I quickly run the groceries in and escape to Dad's to check on him.

"What the hell are you out in this weather for?" Dad says after opening the door.

"Just thought I'd swim over and see how you're doing."

I follow him to the living room and sit beside him on the couch. A Matlock rerun is on TV. Thankfully, he likes Andy Griffith and isn't bitching at the set.

Dad's voice is clear, but still I look around the room for any signs of alcohol. So far, there aren't any empties to be seen.

"Did you hear about the fire out by the Nanaimo River?" he asks suddenly.

"Yeah, some of the locals were talking about it."

"The place was a known drug shack," he says matter-of-factly "I also heard the fire was set intentionally."

"I heard about the suspected drug houses, but nothing about the fire being deliberate. Did you hear that on TV?"

Dad shakes his head. "I called old Marshall, the fella I used to have drinks with at the pub. He said that his pal, Rex, has a son that is a fireman and Rex told Marshall."

"The web of info between the retirees around here is astounding."

"That's right. It's why this is a safe town. Lots of eyes and ears keeping track of the goings on."

"Well, drugs or no drugs, I hope nobody was harmed."

I get Dad a plate of cheese and crackers and a glass of water and sit back down. For a minute or so, we sit in silence while he eats. Then he abruptly hits me with, "Isn't that girl staying at your place a criminal?"

"How did you know that?" I ask, surprised by his knowledge of Jessica's past.

"Your little girlfriend told me."

"She has a name."

"Whatever. Anyways, *Ava* told me her sister hasn't been out of jail that long and she's been staying with the two of you. Is that right?"

I take a deep, silent breath, trying to think of a diplomatic way to answer that won't prompt a lecture from him. "Yes, Jessica got in some trouble a long time ago. She's done her time and has been staying with us until she finds her own place."

"You think that's smart?"

"I don't know, but I bet you're going to tell me why it's not."

"What did she do time for? Drugs? Theft?"

"I don't see how it matters. She's paid for her crimes."

"What were her crimes?"

"Dad, drop it," I say, knowing that he won't.

"I think I have a right to know who's living next door to me."

I groan loudly. "Fine. Not that it matters but, she was incarcerated for arson."

"Ha!" He leans back with his hands on his knees. "Isn't that the biggest coincidence?"

"Coincidence? How do you figure?"

"Did you leave your brains in Vancouver? Think about it, Mila. It's as obvious as the nose on your face."

I find myself wishing that Alex Trebek was on so Dad would have another focus for his snide remarks. "Okay, Dad. Enlighten me with your theory."

"There's never been any trouble in Ladysmith. Just petty crimes. We've certainly never had to worry about arson. Don't you think it's strange that your girlfriend's arsonist sister gets out of the slammer, and all of a sudden there's a house burned down just fifteen minutes from here?"

"No. I don't. It's just a coincidence. Jessica doesn't even have her own car. The river is off the beaten path. It's not logical."

He scoffs. "You're the one not being logical. Mark my words, there's something off about those girls."

I shake my head. "You've got to get a hobby, Dad. Seriously."

* * *

As suspected, when I get to the cabin the two women are at a stand-off, like two cats—backs up, anticipating the attack. The air in the cabin is thick and charged.

Neither one of them says a word to me. It's like my presence has hit a pause button. I say a few words that land on deaf ears, then retire to the safety of my room.

No sooner do I sit than the pause button releases and the verbal spatting begins. Thankfully, I don't live in an apartment. Ava is hollering about Jessica's drug use and carelessness, and Jessica is retorting with claims that Ava owes her and she should mind her own business.

It's a good two hours before the volume in the next room dwindles to a moderate roar, and then turns into muffled conversation I can no longer understand.

Soon after, Ava walks into the bedroom. Her eyes are red and puffy and her cheeks stained with dried tears.

She quietly reiterates the important parts of her fight with her sister, telling me that they've come to a resolution and how Jessica has promised to get help for her drug use. "I'm sure there are people around here that go to Narcotics Anonymous meetings. It shouldn't be hard for her to catch a ride there and back. Hopefully she'll find some friends in recovery that can support her."

I put my arms around her. "That's great news," I say, even though I'm skeptical of Jessica's promise. She's already proven to be untrustworthy. I want to tell Ava not to hold her breath, but I don't. Instead, I ask her if she's hungry, then go into the kitchen and make all three of us a meal from the food Ava and I bought earlier for what was supposed to be a romantic dinner for just the two of us.

* * *

At breakfast, Ava and I sit at the table while Jessica sits on the couch, playing on her phone. Just as we're finishing eating, Jessica pipes up. "I don't believe it, another blaze was lit, this time at a cottage further up the Nanaimo River."

"What?" I ask. "Where did you hear that?"

"It's in the news," she says excitedly. "Apparently someone threw a Molotov cocktail into the bottom window of what was the beginnings of a meth lab. '*Both Nanaimo and Ladysmith sent fire and rescue to put out the raging blaze. One fatality has been reported: a man known to police in Victoria and new to the area. The man was in his early thirties and had a history of trafficking drugs. His local affiliations are unknown—*'"

"Can you stop, please?" Ava interrupts. "I don't want to hear it."

Jessica reads to herself for a moment, then says, "Apparently the house was rented by a man living in Duncan."

"Stop it, Jessica," Ava says louder.

"Ha! Listen to this, the locals even gave their two cents. *'"There have been some shady characters hanging out at the local watering holes," a local resident states. "People are worried our once-quiet town will be overrun by hoodlums."'* This is great! This pissant town needs a bit of shaking up."

Ava gets up from the table, sets her coffee cup hard on the counter and storms into the bedroom, slamming the door behind her.

Jessica lets out a mischievous laugh. With Ava out of earshot, she stays silent as she scrolls on her phone. Wanting to give Ava some time to cool off, I grab my coat and go for a walk at the beach.

As I stroll along the water's edge, I think about what Jessica read and how she got so excited. How she kept reading aloud when Ava pleaded with her to stop. *There's something really wrong with her. Something disturbing.*

Chapter Nine

Don sums the situation up perfectly: "Shit just got real."

For a week, all I hear are whispers and rants about the blaze—theories about why, and who, and when it'll happen again.

At home, the sisters' spats have reached a plateau. There hasn't been an uproar since Jessica antagonized Ava with the news of the fire.

It's a beautiful day, and Ava wants me to come with her to collect small pieces of driftwood and shells from the beach for a mobile she's making. Away from Jessica and the cabin, we spend the afternoon enjoying the outdoors and each other. I have another shift tonight, then in the morning I have to take Dad to see his doctor about the blood tests the mobile lab took from him awhile ago—he hates doctors more than he hates Alex Trebek, so this should be interesting.

* * *

The topic of the fires and the dead man looms over the town like a dark, heavy cloud. After a long night of driving cab, I am more mentally bagged out than I am physically. With any luck, I won't have to hear any more about it until my shift tomorrow night.

With a good night's sleep on my mind, I walk in the cabin and see Ava lying on the couch, almost posing, a faint hint of lavender riding on the air. There are two lit candles on the table and plates filled with what looks to be restaurant pasta.

Ava stands. She's wearing a figure-hugging silver satin nightie, her hair flowing loose over her shoulders.

"Wow. You look stunning." I motion to the table. "Did you do all of this for me?"

She smiles and moves gracefully toward me. Her arms wrap around my neck and she pushes her body against me.

We kiss, soft and slow. Suddenly, I'm not tired anymore. All my senses are waking and I'm getting little electric charges all over my skin.

I pull away a bit. "Where's your sister?"

"She's in Nanaimo, at an NA meeting." She plants another soft kiss on my lips. "She won't be back for hours."

I quickly change into a nightie—not half as sultry and eye-catching as what Ava is wearing—and join her for our dinner. As I eat, she runs her foot up and down my leg, taking my concentration off the meal. Soon, our hands are playing with one another's and we're kissing more than we're eating.

Ava stands up and pulls the thin straps from her shoulders, sending the silk sheath riding over her curves and landing in a bundle around her feet. Before I know it, we're both naked and on the sofa. Hot, sweating and panting, we engulf each other with insatiable hunger. Tasting every bit of each other, we take turns reaching new heights of pleasure until we slump together, gasping and smiling.

"This is what I've missed, Mila. I've missed us feeling like we're one again."

"And now? How do you feel?"

"Satisfied."

We share a shower, laughing and playing, before wrapping in robes and cleaning up the dishes.

We lie embraced in bed. I can tell she's still anxious—she checks her watch every once in a while. Finally, we hear the front door open and Jessica call out, "I know you're still up, listening and wondering if I was going to come home. Well, I'm here. You can go to sleep now, Mom."

Ava and I giggle and drift off to sleep.

* * *

Dad is grimacing and looks pale.

His normal rants have been replaced with long groans as he slouches forward in his wheelchair. I do my best to gently maneuver his emaciated body into the passenger side of my car. Still, I accidently bump into him with the car door. He hollers in pain, then resumes breathing heavily and grunting, not even bothering to yell at me.

All I can think is that I'm glad Mom isn't around to see him like this. It would've torn her apart.

After what feels like the longest ride ever, we arrive at the one level office building downtown. I load Dad into the chair and wheel him up the ramp and into the building. An older receptionist says hello to my father, who only grumbles back. After a few short minutes, she shows us to a room down a short white hallway. Before she closes the door, she asks me if my father is having a lot of pain.

Dad overhears and barks out, "No, it's probably just period cramps."

"Dad," I whisper loudly. "Please behave yourself."

The nurse smiles sympathetically and closes the door.

A while later, Dr. Ryan walks in. He's in his late sixties and has thinning hair the color of fresh snow and a pot belly that his white physician's coat strains to cover. He shakes my hand and tells me that we met at Mom's memorial. I nod politely, as if I remember. Doctor Ryan was Mom's doctor, and my father's since his cancer diagnosis.

"It looks like you're having some pain, John," he says, looking into my father's face. "How bad would you say it is, on a scale of one to ten?"

Dad groans. "About a fourteen."

The doctor pats him on the shoulder and stands. "I'll be right back with something to help with that pain."

I sit in a metal chair across from Dad and look around the small room. One wall has been reserved for plaques, accolades and achievements. Other walls have tacked on them pictures drawn, presumably, by the children he treats.

The doctor walks back into the room, carrying a syringe.

"What's that?" I ask.

"Who gives a shit," my father says. "Just give it to me."

"It's morphine to help John with the pain," Dr. Ryan says, lifting my father's sleeve and giving him the shot. "I'll give that time to work and I'll come back in to see you."

"How long have you been hurting like this?" I ask, once the doctor is out of the room.

He forces a grin. "From about the time you were born."

I giggle. "In major pain and you're still sarcastic."

Dad groans as he tries to shift in the chair. I tell him to sit still until the meds start working. After ten minutes or so, his breathing doesn't seem as labored and he's sitting up straighter. He shifts to get more comfortable.

"Dad, do you need a pillow? Is your butt getting sore?"

"My butt is fine," he says with a slight slur. "But it's funny you should mention *butt*."

"Why is that?" I make the mistake of asking.

"Because I've been thinking a lot about how that's my favorite body part on a woman. I miss lying next to a woman with a great ass. I think you should go on your computer and sign me up for internet dating."

I look at his face to see if he's serious—much to my horror, he is. "Dad, get real."

"I'm not joking. I'm gonna find me a hottie to get busy with. Then she can cook me some good meals. Make sure you put that down—must be a good cook. And the ass, she has to have a good ass, too."

"Well, we know the meds have kicked in."

"It's not the meds. I've been wanting a honey for quite some time now. So do the internet thing for me!" He's getting back the bark he has when he's drunk. "And don't screw it up."

"Okay, Dad. I'll try," I lie. "I just don't know how many blind, deaf, single women there are in the area."

Not a moment too soon, the doctor returns, carrying a file. "Feeling a bit better, John?"

"I'm fine!"

"I've got the results from your last blood test that I want to talk about, but first I'd like to examine you, okay?"

"As long as you don't stick your fingers up my ass again."

"Dad! Stop!"

The doctor seems unphased. He's obviously witnessed this side of my father before.

Dad looks at me and I see the glazed look in his eyes. He's stoned out of his tree. "This guy was hitting on me. Then he stuck his fingers up my ass."

"John," Dr. Ryan says calmly. "I simply gave you a complete physical."

"Yep. That's right. You physically put your fingers up my ass."

"I am so sorry," I say, turning red with embarrassment.

The doctor shrugs, as if to tell me it's no big deal. I offer to help my father change into an examination gown but he protests, saying that he doesn't want me to see his clanking bones. The doctor calls for the nurse and I'm asked to go to the waiting room until the examination is over.

Outside, tiny droplets of water stick to the glass on the small windows. Thankfully, the sky is mostly clear, which means I won't have to worry about maneuvering my stoned-out-of-his-mind dad into the car during a downpour.

Over the next twenty minutes, I hear the odd beller and curse word coming from the examination room, followed by the calm deep voice of the doctor. I shake my head. There's no amount of money that would ever convince me to be a doctor. *The extreme level of crap you'd have to put up with? No thanks.*

Finally, I see the nurse walk out of the room and shut the door. Her face is flushed and her kind disposition has been replaced with an air of frustration as she walks behind the desk and sits in front of a computer. She briefly looks up and says, "The doctor is almost finished with your father."

I smile at her sympathetically.

A few moments later, the doctor walks out and motions for me to come over. When I'm in front of him, he quietly tells me that the blood tests for my dad came back, and the results were bad.

He goes on about how different readings of proteins and blood cell counts are indicators that the cancer has worsened and spread, affecting vital organs. The information is confusing and overwhelming. I wasn't with Dad when they found out he had cancer—this is the first time I've heard it from a medical professional. Even though

I've known my father is sick, to hear it officially knocks the wind out of my chest.

When he's finished speaking, the only words I can muster are, "How long does he have?"

The doctor shrugs, his smile sympathetic. "To be honest, I'm surprised he's lasted this long. Most patients with the same cancer as your father pass on quite quickly. In fact, John is the first of my patients to make it this far."

"It's probably because he pickled his body with alcohol," I say, trying to hide my emotions behind a joke.

The doctor forces a chuckle and tells me that I can take my dad home now.

When I walk into the room, my father is in his chair, his back to me.

I walk up to him. "Everything okay?"

"I'm good." He turns his chair around. "Let's get the hell out of here."

In the car, I ask if the doctor discussed his test results.

"Mila, mind your business," he snaps. "You're not my mother and you're definitely not your mother. You are my kid. If I want you to know about my health, I'll tell you. Don't ask."

"Ok, Prince Charming, as you wish." I start the car. "Can I ask if you're hungry and want to pick up take-out on the way home? Is that okay? Or am I stepping over boundaries again?"

"I don't want food. I want to go home and get my feet up before the pain comes back."

As we drive, Dad turns on the stereo and stares out the window, and my mind wanders as soft tunes play in the background.

I feel sad, really sad, for my father. And for me, too.

I've spent so many years being angry and resentful, I haven't considered how my father's life has changed since Mom died. In the later years, when I was an adult, my parents did everything together. No matter if he was always emotionally unavailable, he loved her.

I glance over at him. He's very thin. If he were standing outside and a gust of wind came, it would probably blow him over. His skin is so drawn and sallow.

He's going to die soon. Maybe not today, or tomorrow, but soon. I've got to come to terms with our past and forgive him. If I don't, I'll pack around the resentment and guilt I feel forever.

"Dammit, Mila," he shouts suddenly. "Can't you keep the car between the lines? Who the hell taught you to drive?"

Usually I'd respond to his nastiness with sarcasm, but I don't feel the desire.

Half an hour after we get back to the cabin, I can tell that Dad's pain is returning. I sit in the chair by the table so he can stretch his spindly legs out on the couch.

Halfway through a Gilligan's Island rerun, Dad drifts off. I switch the TV off, get up and walk toward the door to leave. Just as I grab the handle, he calls my name.

I turn to him. His eyes are half open. "Thank you for everything," he says.

"It's okay, Dad. Sleep now. I'll be back later to check on you."

"Dr. Ryan called in a prescription for pain meds. The pharmacy will deliver them later. I've got my meals coming and that should do me fine. I don't want you to come back today, I just want to take it easy. Come by tomorrow instead."

"Alright, if you're sure. And if something comes up, just call."

* * *

Before I open the door to my cabin, I close my eyes and exhale.

Ava is sure to be up by now, and I don't want her to pick up on my somber mood. It'll only make her feel bad, and I don't want to ruin her day. I force myself to relax before heading inside.

The first thing I see is Jessica. She's sitting on the couch, putting on makeup. Her feet are up on the coffee table, cotton stuffed between each of her toes. The acrid odor of nail polish hits me and I cough.

She glances up from her mirror for a moment. "Hey."

"Hey." I walk past her, holding my breath.

"Ava is in the bedroom."

As soon as I open the door, I see my beautiful girlfriend lying on her stomach, her knees bent and feet crossed behind her. She's writing in her journal, but looks up when I enter. She puts the pen down and brushes her blond locks from her face. "Hi, beautiful. Where have you been?"

"I had to take Dad to his doctor's appointment this morning. You were sleeping so soundly, I didn't want to wake you."

She sits up, looking interested. "How did it go?"

"It went as well as could be expected," I say, trying to keep the discussion light.

"And your dad? How's he feeling about it?"

I smile, appreciating her concern. "Better."

I sit beside her and she closes the journal. "Hey, it's almost noon," she says, glancing at her watch. "Do you want to go to town for some lunch? I'll see if Jessica wants to come."

I nod. She jumps up, stuffing her journal into a small box on the top shelf of the closet before heading into the next room to talk to her sister.

While the two girls buzz around the cabin, getting ready, I lay my head on the pillow and wonder how my father is doing, hoping that his pain isn't unbearable, and praying that he's able to rest.

* * *

The small Italian eatery is more like a diner than a restaurant, with its black and white checkered floor, tall fake trees in the corners, and pictures of food on the walls. This place wasn't here while I was growing up.

The owner and his wife are from China, both are polite and welcoming and speak with thick accents. Jessica almost immediately points out that the owners aren't Italian, and therefore the eatery can't be authentic. Ava asks her to keep her voice down and starts going over the items on the menu with her, much the same way an adult gets a child to behave—by using a diversion.

Both Ava and I decide on the prawn puttanesca while Jessica scrutinizes the dishes on the menu for ten minutes, bitching and moaning about the prices and lack of pictures. Finally deciding on a basic dish of pasta carbonara, she waves the server over and we order.

As the woman collects our menus, Jessica asks for a glass of Chianti. Ava quickly cancels Jessica's drink order and asks for water instead. "You're not supposed to be drinking," Ava reminds her.

"You're such a killjoy." Jessica looks at me. "What do you think about this fire business?" she asks, apropos of nothing.

"I try not to," I respond.

"I think it's kind of funny. I mean, burning down drug shacks? It wouldn't be too hard to find the culprit, if the cops knew what they were doing."

"Why is that?" I ask.

"It's obvious." Jessica unwraps her cutlery. "Some druggie probably got ripped off by a dealer and is seeking revenge." She mimes stabbing with the knife, grinning. "All the cops have to do is put the word out within the drug community."

"There is no drug community here, it's Ladysmith," Ava says.

"There's always a drug community, no matter how small," Jessica retorts. "Drugs are everywhere."

The waitress brings our drinks and sets them on the table.

"What if the arsonist is from Nanaimo?" Jessica muses. "It's only twenty minutes away, and it'd be a lot easier to hide there. It's crawling with drug people."

"Considering a guy died, it's probably not the best conversation to be having over lunch," Ava says shortly.

I nod, grateful that she put a stop to the conversation.

As we eat, Ava talks about a couple of songs she's been working on. I listen with

121

interest, but the boredom is obvious on Jessica's face. It's apparent she has no interest in Ava's music.

After lunch, the three of us grab pastries at the local bakery. Ava, thoughtful as she is, orders a few things for my father that I'll drop off in the morning. I take her hand and give it a squeeze as we leave the bakery.

We eat our dessert on the beach, watching the gentle waves wash on the shore. It's a perfect evening—or would be, if it were just Ava and me.

"I guess we should be heading back," I say after we've finished our pastries. "I start work in a couple of hours."

"You still working that low-man's job?" Jessica says. "Hauling strangers around for a few measly bucks?"

"There's nothing wrong with Mila's job," Ava says. "Or having one in general."

"Aren't you supposed to be looking for work?" I ask, not bothering to be subtle.

"I'm in treatment," Jessica says airily. "Plus, there's dick-all for work here, unless I apply at the fire department. They're probably looking for help right now." She lets out a laugh.

On the drive home, all I can think about is how cold Jessica is. I haven't heard her say one thing to support Ava or encourage her with her music. Everything is about Jessica, and it's really starting to ride on my nerves. She needs to get her shit together, otherwise her stay will be less temporary and more unbearable. If she doesn't get a plan soon, I'll be forced to bring the issue up with Ava, which is the last thing I want to do.

I leave for work not long after getting home. Ava is dedicating the rest of the day to her songs while Jessica finishes doing her nails, as she has an NA meeting in Nanaimo tonight.

As I walk to my car, I look over at Dad's and see the glowing blue flicker of the TV. I want to poke my head in his door just to make sure he's okay, but I can't. I don't want to take away what little control he has left of his life. He asked me not to stop by until tomorrow and, like it or lump it, I've got to abide by his wishes.

When I get to work, Don has loads of news to tell me about the fire. I'm so sick of hearing about it, but he is my boss, so I sit across from him and do my best to look interested.

"They found the guy who had rented the burned house."

"Yeah, I remember hearing about that. He was from Duncan, right?"

"Yes. And a real shyster too, from what I heard. Apparently, the cops caught up to him and he admitted to renting the house, but denied knowing about any drug lab operating there."

"Of course he denied it."

"Yeah, that part didn't surprise me either, but guess what?" Don leans across the desk, his eyes wide. "The guy who died in the fire was this Duncan guy's brother."

I shake my head. "That doesn't help his claim of not knowing anything about the lab, does it?"

"Not at all," Don says.

Thankfully, his computer beeps, signifying a fare. With a smile and a wave, I make my escape out of the building and over to my cab.

After enduring two loud drunks, an overtired screaming child being ignored by its mother, and numerous people from the bingo hall, my shift is completed. With a headache threatening to get worse, I take two aspirin the moment I get into my own car. I drive home, only stopping to get gas and a chocolate bar that Ava texted for me to pick up.

* * *

When I walk through the door, Ava greets me with a warm smile and a plate of leftover dinner she made earlier. We stay up only long enough for me to eat, then head to bed.

About half an hour later, when I'm almost asleep, Ava's phone beeps. She grabs her cell from the nightstand and reads it.

"Who is it?" I ask groggily.

"Jessica. She's running a bit late. She had to wait for her friend to receive their one-year sobriety cake."

"They wait until the end of the meeting to do that?"

Ava shrugs. "I guess so."

I look at the time on my phone. It's past midnight. I don't know much about how NA is run, but something tells me that Jessica is lying.

I don't share my thoughts with Ava. I don't want her pacing the floor until her sister decides to come home.

At what feels like 2AM, I'm awoken to the sound of the front doorknob rattling. I quietly slide out of bed so I don't wake Ava.

As soon as I'm out of the bedroom, I see the cabin door opening and a wobbly Jessica walking in.

"Shh." I press my fingers to my lips. Jessica giggles.. I gently close the bedroom door, then walk over to Jessica. "Be quiet. Your sister is asleep."

"Yeah, well I'm not."

I wince at the stink of alcohol coming from her mouth. "Please just go to bed, Jessica. It's obvious you've been drinking, and I don't want Ava to get up and find you like this."

Jessica teeters in front of me and smiles devilishly. "You're real dumb, you know that? She's got you wrapped around her finger, doesn't she? Baited, hook, line, and sinker."

"I'm not listening to your crap. I just want you to go to bed quietly and sleep it off."

"Is that right?" She cackles. "I hate to throw a wrench into your request, but I'm not staying. You can take your couch, and your tiny little house, and shove them."

"If you leave, your sister will be worried sick."

"That's life. Now, if you'll move out of my way, I'll get my stuff and be gone."

I watch her grab her clothes and things and pile them into her small suitcase. "Where are you going?" I ask. "It's pitch-black outside, and town is a long walk from here."

"Screw this stupid town. My friend is parked outside. I'm taking the first ferry to the mainland. How do you like that?"

"Don't do this. It's a bad move."

She zips up her case and stands up straight. "So was coming here and getting stuck with you two judgemental bitches."

She's gone as fast as she came. As I stand in the doorway, watching the taillights of the car disappear up the dirt road, I think about the impact this will have on Ava. I sigh and slowly close the door.

When I'm back in the room, I look down at Ava. Her breathing is deep and peaceful. I debate waking her, but ultimately decide against it. What does it matter if she gets up now? Jessica is already gone.

Preoccupied with how Ava will react once she finds out, I don't sleep. Instead, I lie still beside her and wait for the sun to come up.

Chapter Ten

Ava slowly wakes as the soft light of morning fills the room. With her eyes half-open, she turns to me and smiles. "Hi beautiful."

I smile and lightly brush her cheek with the back of my hand.

"When did you wake up?" she asks.

"I didn't. I mean, I haven't slept yet."

Ava's eyes open wider. "Why? Are you feeling alright?"

"Fine. I couldn't sleep because I was worried about you."

Ava looks perplexed. "Why? I'm fine."

After taking a deep breath, I sit up. "I got up when I heard Jessica come in last night. She was blitzed out of her mind. Booze this time." I put my hand on Ava's. "She had a plan to leave, and nothing I said would stop her."

"She's not here?" Her voice is suddenly panicked.

"I'm sorry. I tried to talk some sense into her."

She sits up, her face accusatory. "Why didn't you wake me?"

"She was literally here for two minutes, Ava. Just long enough to grab her bag and jump into a car that was waiting outside."

"Did she say where she was going? Or when she's planning on coming back?"

"She mentioned something about going to Vancouver. Then she called us bitches and said we could take this place and shove it."

Ava puts her hand over her face and lets out a frustrated growl. "I've had it. I can't do this anymore." She looks at me. Her eyes are shining with tears. "I had to be interviewed by the parole officer before Jessica was even allowed to come here. If she didn't have this place, she would've had to stay at a halfway house in Victoria. She doesn't care. She just bitched and complained the whole time she was here."

"I know. You are such a caring sister. You don't deserve to be treated this way."

"I'm done, Mila. I'm so done with her. She's never allowed to stay here again, no matter what." There's conviction in her voice that I haven't heard before. But then, the weariness and guilt creeps back. "And now she's violating her restrictions. The parole officer said I needed to call if Jessica broke curfew or took off. I even had to sign something. I have to report her. I have no choice."

I squeeze her hand. "None of this is your fault. Jessica knew the consequences if she messed up. It's on her."

* * *

It's been a long two days of wind and rain, and a combination of sadness and resentment looms over Ava. Thankfully, I can keep her company. One of the part-time drivers is more than happy to pick up my shifts.

Ava has spent the past forty-eight hours in the bedroom, either writing in her journal or working on her shell mobile. I wander in and out of the bedroom, letting her know I'm here if she wants to talk more about Jessica. So far, she hasn't.

Dad has remained diligent in his sobriety, regardless of the overwhelming bouts of pain he suffers with. I'm visiting tonight to see how he's doing. I'm a bit nervous about leaving Ava alone, but there's not much I can do. She declined my offer to come along.

After making an easy salad dinner that Ava poked at with her fork but didn't eat, I put on my rain jacket and boots and head for the door.

Ava stops me before I can leave. "Mila, can I ask you a question?"

I turn to face her. "Of course."

"I haven't been able to call Jessica's parole officer yet. Do you think that I'm weak?"

I shake my head. "No, I don't."

"With every day that passes, I keep telling myself to hold off on calling, in case she comes back." Ava rests her head against the doorframe. "I guess I've been worried that, if I call, she'll be arrested and sent back to jail. I don't want that for her."

"I know you don't."

"But I guess you were right," Ava says with a sigh. "It's her decision to live the way she wants."

I wrap my arms around her. "Are you sure you don't want to come with me to Dad's? I don't feel right leaving you by yourself while you're upset."

Ava looks into my eyes. "I'll be fine. I'm a strong girl. I think it's time I quit moping about and focus on my song writing. And, more importantly, you and me."

I kiss her on the cheek. "I won't be long."

* * *

The blaring TV prevents my father from hearing my knocks on the door. Thankfully it's not locked, so I open it and walk in.

He's sitting in his chair in front of the set, a glass of clear liquid in one hand and the remote control in the other. By the way he's sitting up straight, I can tell that he's not in a

131

lot of pain. He briefly glances over at me, then finishes his drink in one swallow.

"Dad, can you turn the TV down? I can't hear myself think."

He ignores me.

I repeat myself. Again, he doesn't respond. With no other choice, I walk over and stand between him and the set and hold my hand out until he reluctantly passes me the remote.

I turn down the volume. "Why are you blasting it so loud?"

He chuckles. "I only turned it up when I looked out the window and saw you coming."

I shake my head. "Let me guess—you were the kid who burned the wings off flies and dunked girls' ponytails in ink?"

"Naw, the flies were too fast, I couldn't catch them. The girls, on the other hand…"

I smirk. "I honestly don't know how Mom put up with you for so many years."

"It was probably the sex."

"Yuck, Dad. Like I needed that image in my head."

He laughs. "Yep, I was a real stud in the sack."

"If you continue, you're paying for my therapy."

Thankfully, a Jeopardy rerun starts on TV and Dad gets sidetracked. During a commercial, when he wheels to the bathroom, I grab his glass and smell it. Thankfully, it was only water.

I spend the next while gathering laundry as my father curses at Alex Trebek. I'm just stuffing the last of his dirty clothes into a bag when he mutes the TV and calls me over.

"What's up, Dad?" I sit on the couch.

"I want you to stay for a while longer. Don't go home just yet."

"Why? Is something wrong? Are you feeling sick?"

"No, it's nothing like that."

"Then why?"

"Because I don't want you involved in whatever is going on at your place." He points to the window.

I look outside and see two police cars pulled up in front of my cabin.

I jump to my feet. "What in the hell?"

"Sit back down," my father orders. "Wait until they leave."

"When did you notice the cops?"

"A moment before I told you to sit down."

"I have to go over there and see what's going on." I grab my raincoat and pull it on. "I'll come back and tell you what's happening. Or I'll call you."

He shakes his head. "I told you from the beginning. There's something wrong with those girls."

* * *

I don't feel the harsh weather as I leave Dad's and head next door. When I walk in, two officers are standing just inside the door. One is a tall male about fifty, the other a female in her thirties. Both turn to me when I close the door behind me.

Ava is sitting on the couch, looking like a nervous child being questioned by her parents.

"What's going on?" I ask. The male cop asks me my name, then writes it down on the small pad he's holding. I look at Ava. "What's going on?" I ask again.

"They're here about Jessica."

The female cop studies me. "Jessica is unlawfully at large. She has breached her parole conditions."

"Oh," I say, trying to sound clueless. "Well, she's not here."

"I already told them the last time we saw her," Ava says. "And where she said she was going."

I walk past the officers and sit beside Ava on the couch. The officers ask a few more questions, then tell us to notify them if Jessica contacts us or we hear where she is. The woman hands Ava her card, and they leave.

"Wow. That was unexpected," I say.

"Not really." Ava stands and sticks the card on the fridge with a magnet. "I knew it was only a matter of time before they showed up."

"Are you okay?"

Ava nods, still facing away. "Though the thing that kind of rattled me was…was…"

"What?"

She turns to look at me. "Well, they asked me if I could tell them anything about the fires."

I feel, all of a sudden, cold. "Weird. I wonder why?"

She shrugs. "It makes sense when you think about it." She rubs her face and heads toward the bedroom. "There's no way she lit the fires. But she was arrested for arson. Of course they'd ask."

* * *

For the past two hours, Ava has been lying in bed. I know I've got to get her out of here, at least for a while. It's the only thing that'll snap her out of her somber mood.

I walk into the bedroom and sit beside her. "Sweetie, I know you're feeling awful, but I really need your help."

She groans. "With what?" she answers weakly.

Thinking fast, I say, "I've got to pick up a new mattress. For Dad. And I can't lift it by myself."

"Mattress? How are you going to transport a mattress? Your car's tiny."

"I know. I…I'm going to strap it to the roof."

She looks up at me with skepticism. "Why can't the mattress place just deliver it?"

Recognising the obvious holes in my story, I cough a few times into my arm, using the brief moment to think of what to say next. "The...the mattress store in town can't deliver until next week, and my father needs it now."

Wearily, she sits up. "Okay. I'll come."

As she slowly makes her way to the bathroom, I quickly try and figure out where to take her. I grab my phone and search for things to do on the Island. When the list of attractions close by pops up, the first thing I see is bungee jumping. I quickly scroll past it.

I hear the water in the bathroom sink shut off just as I scroll past a colourful ad. I scroll back up, and a grin spreads across my face.

* * *

Instead of turning into town, I take the freeway northbound.

"I knew it!" Ava exclaims, glaring at me. "I knew you were just bullshitting. Your dad doesn't need a mattress. You just wanted me out of the house."

Thankfully, she doesn't look truly mad. I can see a smile hiding. "Sorry," I say.

"You're such a brat!" She switches on the stereo.

Majestic firs line the narrow road that winds along the shore. Tofino is truly a hidden gem. Surfers, nature enthusiasts, and artists convene there year-round.

As I pull into town, Ava points to a wooden tribal eagle covering the front of a large building. "It's a museum. I'd love to go in if we have time."

It's the first time in days that I've seen her show any enthusiasm. "Yeah, we can definitely try. But we'll have lots to see where we're going."

I pull up to the small building at the bottom of the road. Ava jumps out and looks up at the sign. *Whale Watching.* She turns to me, her face shining. "You're taking me on a boat?"

Inside, we speak to the kind girl behind the desk, who tells us that the next whale watching tour is in a half hour.. After we sign a waiver and pay, the woman produces two sets of rain resistant jumpsuits and gloves, which we opt to leave in the office until it's time to board.

To kill time, we walk a few doors down to the Coffee House. Beautiful fresh pastries are stacked behind a glass counter that Ava and I visually devour. As we're ordering our coffees, Ava almost buys a couple of donuts before I caution her that a bumpy boat ride on the ocean isn't the best place to have a full stomach. With our coffees, we sit at the small table nearest the window.

"I love the warmth of this place," she says, looking dreamily out the window. "One day I'd love to live in a small seaside place like this. I feel miles away from the noise and crowds of bigger towns. I think I'd be able to write songs with a lot more freedom if I lived here, in the middle of nature."

I gaze at her, so happy she's loving the vibe here. You'd never guess that just a few hours ago she was so depressed, I could barely get her out of bed.

After finishing our coffees, we head back to the whale watching office, where two other couples wearing the rain gear are gathered. After Ava and I get our jumpsuits on, all of us are led down a dock to where a Zodiac-style open boat is tied.

When everyone is secured in their seats, our guide stands at the helm behind us and slowly motors out of the bay. The water is as still as glass as we sail between two tiny islands covered with craggy trees and foliage. The gentle sea wind rushes over us and lifts our hair. Ava looks over at me and mouths, *This is incredible.*

I reach over and squeeze her hand.

Soon, all land disappears and the boat speeds up as we head into open water. With no shelter from land, swells form, making the small craft bump and jerk. I'm reminded of being on a ride at the fair. Everyone grips onto the sides as the waves grow. Ava is laughing from the sensation, and tears from the wind leave wet streaks on her cheeks.

After about a half hour, the boat slows and the wind eases, letting us hear the guide.

He points to a spot on the water. "Watch. It's a humpback."

At first, nobody sees anything. Then I spot something dark under the surface. It's a small dorsal fin. Only half of the people on board see it before it completely disappears. Ava looks disappointed, and I squeeze her hand again.

The guide puts the engine in neutral and we all continue staring at the same spot. The minutes tick past.

Then, after about ten minutes, Ava lets out a small gasp. "Hey, what's that?" She's looking down into the dark water just over the edge of the boat. I lean over to see what she's looking at.

As I peer into the dark sea, I notice what looks like a large stone getting bigger. There are small, roundish spots on top of the dark background.

The guide notices us focussing on something and looks himself. "Hey," he says to the group, "It's a whale, and it's right alongside us."

The boat tips slightly as the other passengers lean to get a glimpse. Sure enough, the rock-like blob rises closer to the surface.

"It's massive, Mila," says Ava under her breath, as the rest of the enormous creature appears parallel to the boat. The white spots I saw are barnacles stuck to the whale's head. "This is incredible."

"Is it safe to be so close to such a huge whale?" one of the female passengers asks the guide nervously.

"We'll be fine. They don't hang around for too long."

Ava and I watch intently as the magical creature turns onto its side, revealing one of its eyes.

"He's checking us out," I giggle.

There are murmurs of complaint from a couple of people about not being able to see the creature. The guide promptly tells them to be patient.

Ava lowers her fingers into the water just above the whale. "I wish I could touch it."

The whale slowly fades as it sinks deeper into the depths. Both Ava and I sigh.

"It's gone," the guide says. "We'll go up a ways and see if there are any more nearby."

He doesn't even put the boat into gear before something dark flashes in front of us, and we collectively gasp.

No more than fifty feet away, the goliath creature breaches high out of the water. It towers over us before landing with a huge splash that sprays water over the boat.

Everyone cheers and hollers at the gift of witnessing the whale so close. Ava taps my leg and I look over at her. "I love you, Mila." Her eyes are shiny.

The euphoria I felt seeing the whale quickly vanishes, immediately replaced with a feeling that comes from deeper inside me. Nervous and excited, I muster my courage. "I love you too."

The rest of the sightseeing tour doesn't disappoint. A group of porpoises ride and frolic in the wake of the boat, and we even see huge sea lion resting on the rocky shore of a small island. Just as we pull back into Tofino, the guide points up at the top of a giant tree, where a large bald eagle sits and scans the earth below.

Ava takes my hand as we make our way back to the car. "It was the best day ever."

I grin warmly back at her, replaying the words that she said to me while we were on the boat. "I agree. And I love you."

"I love you too."

* * *

Wrapped in a euphoric bubble, Ava and I talk, laugh, and make love well into the early hours of the morning.

After getting just enough sleep to function, I get dressed and go next door to check on Dad. As soon as I walk inside, I can tell he's pissed about something.

Armed with my happy mood, I'm feeling confident that I can repel any negativity he spits at me. "Good morning, Dad. How are you today?"

"What the hell are you so happy about?" he grumbles.

I shrug, still smiling. "Just life, I guess."

"Well, stop it. It's annoying."

I chuckle. "Why so venomous?"

"I guess because you promised to let me know why the police were at your place. You never called."

"Oh, that's right. I'm sorry. Time just got away from me."

"So? Are you going to tell me or what?"

"The cops were there looking for Jessica. She breached her parole."

"Not surprised."

I look by the table and see the laundry bag I had meant to take with me and wash. "I'll drop off your clothes at the laundromat on my way to work this evening, ok?"

He nods.

Then wanting Dad to share in some of my happiness, I ask him if Ava and I can make him dinner tonight. "We can all sit for a meal and have a good visit."

He looks up at me. "I can't control who you choose to associate with, Mila." There's a serious tone to his voice that I don't hear often. "But I don't want the likes of your girlfriend or her sister coming over here again." I can tell from his expression that won't be moved on the subject.

I feel a flash of anger. "You're being unreasonable," I say, trying to keep my voice even. "You're missing out on getting to know a great girl."

"Just because you're too blind to see what kind of person she is, doesn't mean I am."

Normally when he's this pigheaded, I'd snap back. But I don't want his negative energy to poison my good mood, so I quash the dismay I feel. "Alright then, have it your way."

I don't stay long. After attending to his needs and putting the laundry in my car, I head back to my cabin to see Ava. I push away my father's words and spend the remaining hours before I have to leave for work cuddled on the couch with my girl.

Chapter Eleven

The lady at the laundromat is sweeping up and getting ready to close when I walk in with the bag of Dad's dirty clothes. She takes the bag from me then tells me that I can pick it up tomorrow afternoon.

Don seems to be in a joyful mood when I walk into his office. He's smiling and animated as he speaks on the phone. When he hangs up, he looks at me with a grin still on his face. "I'm glad you're back. I had a few calls where people requested you."

I laugh. "Wow, I'm famous."

"Things have been really busy lately. I think people are starting to feel safe again now that all that fire business has seemed to stop."

"Good. I just hope I don't have to listen to a bunch of people talking about it still. It was starting to depress me."

"I don't blame you. I'm sure the folks around here are tired of it, too."

Ava and I text each other back and forth through the night, which makes my shift go by quicker. Thankfully, the subject of Jessica doesn't come up. I'm sure Ava thinks about her, but she's no longer Ava's sole focus. I couldn't be happier.

On my last fare of the night, Don messages me to pick up a guy from in front of the bar on First Street. *Another request for you, by name! You really are famous.*

I snort at the message. Good thing I'm the only driver working right now. I pull out and head toward First Street.

Standing in the shadows, leaning against the brick wall outside the bar, is a guy in his early thirties. His light brown, shoulder-length hair falls in strings around his face. He's puffing on a cigarette and playing with what looks to be a small pocketknife.

I don't recognise him, which is odd, considering he'd requested me by name.

Maybe it's not even the guy. I pull up and unroll the passenger side window. "Did you call for a cab?"

He glances up at me and grins before folding the knife and slipping it into the front pocket of his jeans. Slowly, he walks to the cab and gets into the backseat.

I look into the rear-view mirror for longer than usual, trying to find something familiar about him that would warrant the request he made through dispatch. "Where to?" I ask, still looking at him.

He waits a few beats, then chuckles. "Now that is the question, isn't it?" he says lazily.

What the hell is this guy's deal? Alarm bells are going off in my head. Everything is telling me not to drive anywhere. To order him out of my cab.

A loud blare from a car horn blasts behind the cab. Without thinking, I pull away from the curb and start driving.

"Where to?" I ask again, making my voice stronger and louder.

"Just drive around the block."

As we cruise down the street, I keep my eyes on him when I can. He's watching me, too. The light from the streetlamps illuminates his pale skin, giving his face a sinister look.

My pulse quickens and my heart pounds as I turn down the next street. When I glance in the mirror next, I see the stranger reach into his pocket and pull out the small knife.

My chest constricts, making it hard to draw a breath. I watch as he opens the blade and examines it, the lights from outside shining off the steel.

Just two more quick turns, and we're back to the bar entrance. He uses the tip of the knife to pick under his fingernails while his eyes stay transfixed on mine in the mirror.

I want to ask him who he is, and how he knows my name. I know I've never seen him before. I've seen a lot of people while driving cab, but I never forget a face—especially one like his. Still, I say nothing.

Finally, I round the last corner and turn down the street toward the bar. Other people are gathered in a huddle as we pull up to the entrance.

The man lets out a long breath and, knife in hand, leans over the seat closer to me. I cringe away slightly, my fingers white on the wheel.

"I'm glad we got a chance to meet, Mila." He flicks a ten-dollar bill over the seat. Then, finally, he gets out.

I immediately pull away. Even though I'm driving, I hit the automatic door locks.

Back at the cab stand, I hand the keys to Don. He frowns at my hand, which I only notice now is shaking hard. "Did something happen?" he asks, concern on his face.

"I don't know. I just had a weird fare."

I briefly describe what happened, and Don looks sympathetic. "Yeah, you get weirdos sometimes. They're rare, but they happen. You're okay, though, right?"

"I guess so. But he knew my name and requested me, which is weird because I've never seen the guy before tonight."

Don puts his hand on my shoulder. "It's a small town, Mila. I'm sure everyone knows your name by now. Don't let this creep get under your skin. He was probably just trying to freak you out."

Even though his words make sense, something tells me there's more to it. By the way the stranger leered at me, I could just tell that his motivation was personal.

I take the long way home, trying to shake off any residual nerves from my creepy interlude. Like Don, Ava would notice my shaking hands, and she'd worry about my safety driving cab. I don't want or need that kind of energy between us. Not now.

* * *

My cellphone's ringtone wakes me out of a deep sleep. I grab the phone from the nightstand and answer it. It's Don, asking me to fill the afternoon shift—the day guy is ill and won't be coming in. I agree, thinking that it would be nice to spend some time with Ava in the evening for once.

Since I'll no longer be free in the afternoon, I ask if Ava can pick up Dad's laundry for me and just leave it in the trunk of her car until I get home from work. She gladly agrees, and I'm thankful she doesn't offer to take the laundry inside. The last thing I want is to explain that she's not welcome in my father's cabin anymore.

Even though it's daytime, I'm still feeling a bit nervous about the guy that got into my cab last night. I remind myself that even if the guy tried to get into my cab again, there are a lot more people out during the day. There's no way the creep would cause me trouble with so many witnesses around.

After a busy spell of fares, there's a lull in calls and I'm able to grab something to eat. I park on the street in front of a bakery and run inside for a coffee to go and a sandwich.

As soon as I'm back in my car, a fare comes up on my screen. A pickup on the other side of town. I take a few sips of my drink, stick it in the cupholder, then pull onto the road.

I'm just about to turn north onto Dogwood Drive when I see Ava at the gas station across the street—likely grabbing gas after picking up Dad's laundry. I tap the horn a couple of times to get her attention, but she doesn't hear me.

About five minutes later, I reach my location: a three-story walk-up with two senior ladies hanging onto walkers at the entrance.

They're headed to the same bakery I was just at. On the drive, the women discuss a man who apparently lives in their building who "everyone has the hots for." From what I can make out, the man is a lot younger than them—only 81. I chuckle to myself all the way down Douglas Street.

When we turn past the gas station on the corner, I'm surprised to see Ava's car still there. As I wait at a red light, I see her and a man come from inside the station and walk toward her vehicle. *Who the hell is with her?* I consider honking my horn again, but I don't. Instead, I just watch.

Ava opens her car door and the man walks up behind her. She turns to face him.

Suddenly, a cold chill passes through my body. I remember the creep from last night, and I can see the uncanny resemblance to the guy standing just inches from my girlfriend.

Cars honk behind me, and I realize the light has turned green.

The rest of the way to the bakery, I'm in a complete daze. I wonder if Ava knows the man, or if he saw her for the first time and followed her to her car.

The logical part of me says that I'm just paranoid—that it likely wasn't even the same man, and my nervous brain had merely projected onto some random stranger.

The other part of my brain is screaming at me, telling me I should have stopped, regardless of my fare. That I was crazy for leaving Ava with the man.

At the bakery, the elderly ladies are slow to get out of the backseat and onto the curb. With thoughts of rushing back to the gas station, I quickly get their walkers out of the trunk. For what seems like forever, the two women haggle about which one will pay the fare. Finally, one of them holds out the money, which I all but snatch from her hand before jumping back into the cab and firing up the motor.

Driving as fast as I safely can, I make my way back to the gas station. I pull into the parking lot and drive to where Ava was parked, but she's gone.

I quickly pull my phone out of my pocket and dial her. Almost immediately, the call goes to voicemail. I hang up and tap out a text, telling her to call me asap.

For the last hour of my shift, I'm preoccupied with checking my phone whenever possible. Ava doesn't text back.

* * *

When I pull up to the cabin, I'm relieved to see her car. My relief is promptly followed by a wave of frustration.

When I walk in, she's sitting on the couch, reading a book. She looks up at me and smiles. "Hi. How was your day?"

"Interesting."

She closes the book. "Oh yeah? Tell me about it?"

"Well, at one point I was passing by the gas station and I saw you."

"Oh really?"

"Yeah. There was someone else with you. A man."

The smile slides off her face. Suddenly, she looks uncomfortable. "I was at the gas station. I only stopped for a few bucks in gas. I don't know what guy you're talking about— I didn't meet anyone. That's crazy."

"Really?" I sit next to her. She picks at the cover of her book, not looking at me.

151

"Because I wasn't far away and I know what I saw. You weren't even at the pumps. You were in the lot. You and this man left the building together, and you both stopped and talked beside your car."

I'm not sure if it's because I have too many details that she can't keep up the lie, or if she actually only just remembered, but suddenly she says, "Oh, I know what you're talking about. I went inside to grab the receipt for the gas, because the pump didn't give me one, and there was a guy inside. He followed me to my car and asked if I had any money to spare. I told him I didn't, and then he walked away."

Despite the confidence in her tone, she's still not making eye contact.

Not wanting to push the issue, I go into the bedroom to change out of my work clothes. Ava follows me and sits on the bed. Obviously wanting to change the subject and cut the tension in the air, she holds up the book she's reading. "I love Stephen King, don't you? I've been reading his novel, The Body, and—"

"Ava," I interrupt. "I didn't tell you this the other night because I didn't want you to worry. But the man I saw you with today is the same guy who got into my cab and scared the hell out of me."

As Ava listens wide-eyed, I describe how the guy took out a knife to intimidate me, how he cleaned his nails with the tip, and how he had no destination in mind, only wanting to go around the block. "And the strangest part was," I finish, "he requested me by name. I've never met him in my life, and he knew who I was."

Ava is quiet for a few moments. I can tell that she's worried and racking her brain. "That's so strange," she says. "He didn't say anything about you at all. He just asked for some spare cash. What a weird coincidence."

"I'll say." I slide on a pair of jeans and a t-shirt before sitting beside her on the bed. "Ava, I need you to promise me something, okay? Our relationship depends on it."

She meets my gaze.

"Promise me that no matter how much you feel something would upset me, you'll always tell me the truth."

She nods. "You are the most important person in my life. I will never lie to you, Mila."

We hug, but it feels different than usual. As if there's a thick piece of glass between us.

I stand. "I should probably run Dad's laundry over to him. Where did you put the bag?"

"It's in the trunk of my car," she answers. "I'll get it."

"It's ok, I'll just grab it on my way next door."

"No. Just wait and I'll bring it in."

Ava jumps up and heads into the living room. She's just slipping on her shoes when her phone rings. She pulls it out and checks the screen, and her face lights up. "It's Jessica's parole officer," she says excitedly. "Maybe they've found her."

She presses the phone to her ear., Not wanting to wait, I mouth the words, "I'm going to Dad's." She nods, distracted by the call.

As she talks on the phone, I slip on my shoes and grab her keys from the table. Outside, I pop the trunk of her car and grab the laundry bag. I'm just about to close the hatch when I see a smaller bag in the back of the trunk. I reach in and grab it, thinking maybe the lady at the laundromat used two bags when packing Dad's clothes. However, as soon as I open the bag, the strong odors of gasoline and lavender hit me.

Holding my breath, I pull out a long, purple sweater, much like the one Jessica wore while she was here.

For a long moment I just stand there, holding the sweater. I debate going inside with it, asking Ava what it was doing in her trunk, and why it smelled so strongly of gas. In the end, I stuff the sweater back into the bag and put it back where I found it.

* * *

As soon as I walk in the door, Dad sniffs and makes a face. "What did you do, bathe in gas?" he asks.

I set his laundry down and go to the sink to scrub my hands. "I just spilled some on my hands at the gas station."

After putting my father's laundry away, I join him on the sofa. A picture of Mom is sitting on the end table beside him.

"Where did you find that?" I ask, pointing at the photo.

He sighs. "It was in the small chest in the closet." He grabs it and hands it to me.

"She looks so healthy and beautiful," I say, studying the picture. "When was this taken?"

"When she was younger than you are now. We'd just arrived in Victoria and were walking on the grounds in front of The Empress Hotel. I remember thinking how lucky I was to have this beautiful creature beside me. So, I took out my camera and snapped the picture to remember the moment."

I'm not used to my father being so sentimental and open. It temporarily leaves me speechless.

"Mila, I wasn't always a good husband to her. She could've done a lot better for herself than to hook up with the likes of me. Over the years, I never understood why she stayed with me. Could be why I was sometimes a bastard. I figured I'd give her a reason to leave, but she never did."

I catch a glimpse of a tear before he quickly wipes it away.

"Dad, maybe we shouldn't be talking about this if it's making you upset," I say softly.

"Yeah. What's the difference now, anyway? It is what it is. In the end, she did leave me. She left us both."

Feeling uncomfortable and unsure what to say next, I change the subject. "Have you eaten yet?"

"No. I looked at the food they delivered. If you can call it food." His tone was returning to its normal sarcasm "It looked like someone already ate it."

I laugh. "That's gross. Why don't I see what you have in the cupboards and whip you up something?"

"Do what you want," he says, switching on the TV.

A can of tomato soup, a sticky, half-full container of honey and an ancient looking packet of soda crackers is all I can see in the small cupboards.

"Hey, Dad, how old are the crackers?"

"How the hell should I know? Isn't there a date on them?"

I turn the package over and see the stamp. "It says it expired two years ago so I'm thinking we should pass."

Dad chuckles and shakes his head. "Sarcasm. You're a chip off the old block."

I heat up the can of soup and set it on the table beside him. He hands me the remote and I scroll through the channels, briefly stopping on a Hallmark movie just to hear his reaction. ("Mila. Use your damn head. I am not watching this sappy shit. Turn it!")

Finally, I settle on a black and white movie, *Some Like it Hot*, starring Marilyn Monroe, Tony Curtis, and Jack Lemmon.

For the next hour and a half, we laugh our asses off as Tony Curtis and Jack Lemmon dress in drag, pretending to be women. At one point, my father is laughing so hard, he starts choking.

When the credits roll, I gather his dishes, wash them, then tell him I'll see him tomorrow. As I head for the door, he says, "Thanks for not trying to feed me the fossilized crackers. I probably would've deserved it if you did."

I briefly turn to him. "I had a good time tonight, Dad."

* * *

Ava greets me at the door. "I was just going to go next door to see what happened to you. You're never gone this long."

"Sorry, we watched a movie."

She smiles, then walks to the stove, where some kind of canned soup is heating up in a pot.

"So." I sit at the table. "How was your call with the parole officer? Did they find Jessica?"

She shakes her head. "They just called to see if I'd heard anything."

"I'm sorry they didn't have news. I hope the call didn't make you start worrying again."

"I'm fine." She shrugs. "Like you said. It's her life."

I nod sympathetically. "Oh, before I forget, I think Jessica's sweater is in your trunk. I thought maybe the bag had something of Dad's clothes in it, so I opened it. I was almost blown over by the gas smell."

Ava stops stirring whatever is in the pot. "Yeah, I know. I found it on the side of the cabin when I went for a walk to the beach. I didn't know what to do with it, so I put it in my trunk."

"Don't you think it's weird that it reeks of gas?"

"I do. I don't know what to make out of it." Several more moments pass as she stirs. "I feel bad for saying this...but as soon as I smelled that sweater, I thought of the fires on the Nanaimo River."

"You don't think Jessica had something to do with them, do you?"

She turns to me with a glum expression. "I don't know. The more I think about it, and the time frame that the fires occurred, the more I can see how she could have done it."

I'm shocked at what Ava is telling me. She's usually so tight-lipped when it comes to Jessica. For her to actually think that her sister could be responsible for the blazes that caused a man's death…

"But I have no evidence, except for the stinky sweater." Her shoulders slump. "So, what difference will my opinion make?"

I stand up and walk to her. "Look at me, Ava."

With a wooden spoon in her hand, she turns and looks into my eyes.

"What does your gut tell you? Do you think she's responsible for the fires?"

Her eyes are blazing. "All I know is that there was no mention of arson before she got out of jail. Everything happened when she came to live with us, which is only fifteen minutes from where the fires took place. And it's a little hard to dismiss the fact that she split in the middle of the night and left town. If she is innocent, why would she jeopardize her freedom like that?"

"But how would she get to the Nanaimo River? And what would her motive be?"

"I've been thinking about that. The fires were started at night, right?"

I nod.

"Both times there was a blaze, Jessica was late coming home. The first time she said she was hanging out with a friend and lost track of time. The second time was when she came home hours late from supposedly attending an NA meeting."

I exhale deeply. "That's heavy, Ava. Are you going to bring this up with her parole officer?"

"Why? What's the point? I'm just presuming. And I'm pretty sure that won't hold water legally."

I shake my head. "I don't know what to say."

"There's nothing you can say. I guess we'll just have to wait to see what unfolds."

She sounds strong and resilient, but I know she's just putting up a front. I've seen her and Jessica together. I know how much she cares for her sister.

Chapter Twelve

Ava runs into the bedroom and jumps on the bed, waking me up. "Mila, guess what? I've got a gig playing in Nanaimo at the Bastion Street Lounge tomorrow night. It's nice and close, so I won't have to spend the night away from you."

I sit up and rub my eyes. "That's great. Unfortunately, I can't come and watch you. I'll be working."

Ava shows a brief moment of disappointment, then resumes her enthusiasm. "You know, I've really missed playing to a live crowd. I think this'll be really good for me. It'll clear my head."

"Well, I'm happy for you."

On my way to the shower, my cell rings. It's my father.

"Hello?"

I can hear him on the other end. He's trying to tell me something, but his breathing is labored, and I can't understand him.

I hang up, then quickly put on pants and a shirt. As I slip on my shoes and grab my coat, I tell Ava that my father is in trouble, and I'll call her when I know what's going on.

* * *

My father is sitting at the table when I walk in. His head is resting on his arms.

"Dad, are you okay? What's happening?"

He groans. "The pain. It's bad."

A wave of panic hits me. "I'm going to call the ambulance."

He lifts his head. His eyes are strained and squinting. "No! I don't want the damn ambulance. I want you to take me to the hospital."

I quickly get him loaded in his wheelchair, then dash out the door to my car. I back up so the passenger door is easily accessible.

I spot Ava looking at us out the window. Ten seconds later, she runs out the door and helps me maneuver Dad into the passenger seat.

"What's she doing here?" he protests.

"Dad, she's helping, don't worry about it."

I thank Ava, then tell her I'll text her from the hospital in Nanaimo. Unfortunately, Ladysmith only has an urgent care center—something between a hospital and a walk-in clinic. There are no overnight stays and they close at the end of the day. Thankfully, Nanaimo is only a twenty-minute drive.

Once at the highway, I turn Northbound and put my foot down hard. My father is slumped over and groaning, with his head resting on the window.

"Dad, hang in there. I'm going as fast as I can." I put my hand on his shoulder.

He flinches at my touch. "Don't bloody well coddle me. I'm not a child."

As soon as we arrive at the Emergency entrance, I run through the automatic doors and tell the nursing staff that I need help getting my father out of the car. In no time, there are two large male orderlies lifting Dad out of the car and onto a stretcher.

After parking the car, I go inside to where my father is waiting in a room to be examined. He's lying on his side toward me. Under the bright, unforgiving fluorescent lights, I see how the illness has ravaged his weak, emaciated body. His eyes are closed and his face is an ashen color. If it wasn't for his labored breathing, I would think he was dead.

When I first returned to the Island, I had a shield around me that took years to build. No matter what, I wasn't going to let him hurt me emotionally anymore. But the more time I spent with him, the more things changed. My shield disappeared without me knowing it. Now, I feel exposed and vulnerable.

I don't want him to die. I'm just getting to know him as an adult.

He has his quirks and his meanness, but now I realize that his outbursts have nothing to do with me and everything to do with his own guilt and regrets. He was right, not just about me being like him sarcastically. I'm like him because we both try to deflect how we're feeling on the inside. As hard as it is to fathom, I think I'm more like him than I am my mother.

Two hours later, Dad has been seen by the doctor, had blood tests taken and is hooked up to an I.V. After the tests come back, the doctor walks in and tells us that Dad will be admitted until they can sort out his medications. The doctor's words aren't as scary as my father's unusual reaction to the news; he is fine with being admitted. I hope this isn't a sign of him giving up.

I'm in a daze for the whole drive back to the cabin. I know I can't change things and heal my father. Like his family doctor said, my dad has outlived other patients with the same type of cancer. I just want him to stay with me a while longer. I want to collect more good memories that'll stay with me long after he's gone. I grip the steering wheel and glance up in between the clouds at the blue sky. "Please, God, please let me keep him for just a while longer."

At home, Ava suggests I call Don and cancel my shifts for the next few days until I know what's happening with Dad. I hadn't even thought about work since I left the hospital.

I call my boss and tell him my situation. He reassures me that my shifts will be covered and to take as much time as I need.

Ava heats up a store-bought pasta dish, which I barely eat. I call the hospital and discover they've moved my dad to the cancer ward on the main floor. I ask the nurse if I should come back today, and she tells me that my dad is sleeping. The last thing I want to do is disturb him if he's resting and not in pain.

When dinner is over, Ave sits on the couch, writing up setlists for her gig, and I'm doing my best not to worry.

After an hour or so of twiddling my thumbs, I grab my jacket and tell Ava I'm going for a walk on the beach.

* * *

It's a clear and peaceful evening as the last of the day lingers in the West. Like an orange fireball, the sun drops from the sky and extinguishes in the sea.

I walk on the sand along the shore before coming to a small, hollowed-out log, where I sit. Looking up at the sparkling flutters of stars, I silently pray that my dad's pain eases so he can be here with me, even for just a while longer. I'm not ready to be an orphan yet. Now that we've reconnected, there are too many things I want to say to him. Things that involve forgiveness and acceptance. The problem is, when I'm in front of him and he's being callous and cold, I get into defense mode, and all the things I want to tell him disappear.

Regardless, I don't have much time. I've got to try my hardest to speak my truth. For his sake, and for mine.

I'm so grateful that I met Ava and I meant what I said to her in Tofino. I do love her, but the love for a parent is different. No matter how dysfunctional the relationship, you have a magnetic pull to them. I'm afraid when my father dies, I'll lose all connection to who I am.

I wait another half an hour before the wind picks up and it's time to go home.

I come home to find that Ava has run me a bath, and has her lavender-perfumed candles strategically placed around the small bathroom. Though I'm not feeling into it, I get undressed anyway. I don't want to hurt her feelings.

Once I'm in the steamy water, Ava disrobes and slips in with me. I'm not in a romantic mood, regardless of how perfect her naked body is.

Ava grabs the sponge on the side of the tub and soaks it in the water before slowly squeezing it over my neck and shoulders. Instantly, the hot water starts to relax me.

She repeats the action over and over until the tension in my muscles eases. I fight hard to keep my eyes open.

I'm nearly asleep when Ava finally gets out. I watch her dry off with a towel, then run naked into the bedroom to get my housecoat. "Thanks, Ava," I call softly.

Her soft, beautiful voice floats back. "You're welcome."

* * *

The warm sound of a guitar gently rouses me from my sleep. Ava is playing in the next room. I sit up and immediately think of Dad, and my stomach clenches as I wonder how he's doing this morning. I remind myself that he's in a hospital and surrounded by medical staff who will do everything they can to make sure he's not suffering.

In the front room, Ava is sitting on the couch, playing her guitar. I walk over and sit beside her. After a few songs, she stops and leans the guitar on the couch before turning to me, her face serious.

"Are you okay?" She looks deep into my eyes.

"I think so. I mean, there's not much I can do to change my father's condition. I just have to go along with whatever happens, as shitty as that may be."

The morning is busy. I go next door briefly to pack a bag for Dad, grabbing anything he might need for his stay at the hospital: a razor, a hairbrush, pajamas. Meanwhile in our cabin, Ava buzzes around, getting ready for her gig this evening.

"What time are you going to the hospital to see your dad?" she asks, making tea.

"I should probably go soon. I want to be there when the doctors do their rounds so I can find out what's going on with him. He certainly won't tell me."

"And do you think you'll be stopping by the lounge to watch one of my sets when you're done at the hospital?"

"I don't think so. Something tells me I won't be in the best frame of mind after." I sigh, taking the cup of tea Ava holds out for me. "I'll probably just come home and defragment."

Ava nods. "I understand."

I give her a quick kiss. "Good luck tonight, by the way."

"I'll be thinking of you."

* * *

Hospitals are depressing places where the sick and injured sit in chairs or lie in beds, waiting to be treated. As soon as the automatic glass doors open, I hear moans of discomfort and pain as the thick odors of industrial cleaner and sickness surround me.

When I walk up to the nursing desk to find out where my father is, I'm directed through the heavy metal doors that lead to the cancer unit.

Long white hallways branch off from a glass-encased nurses' station. I feel like I'm in a maze. I walk up and wait a few moments before a portly nurse with a tight perm and thick glasses approaches me.

"Excuse me," I ask. "Which room is John Dovey in?"

She smiles and leads me to a medium-sized room with four beds separated by curtains. I follow her to the corner bed, my heart thumping hard. She pulls back the curtain.

Much to my surprise, Dad is sitting up with a tray of food in front of him. He glances up and grins. "There's my brat."

The nurse leaves us and I pull a chair up beside the bed. "How ya feeling?"

"Compared to being hit by a Mack truck, I'd say I'm doing great, but compared to how I'd like to feel, not the best."

I nod. "Have they told you what's going on with you since you've been here?"

Dad gives me a serious look. "Yeah. You're not going to believe it, but apparently, I have cancer."

I shake my head. "You're such an ass."

It's only later when my father is wheeled into the shower room down the hall that I can sneak up to the nursing station to speak with the doctor between his rounds.

A young physician tells me that my dad is in the end stage of his disease and their sole motivation is to keep him comfortable. The doctor spoke to my father about going into palliative care, and the idea was strongly rejected. "I think your father wants to spend whatever time he has left at home. If that's workable for you, I can write up a drug schedule to help manage his pain and other symptoms. We'll get him stabilized over the next few days, then you can take him back home."

The doctor is called away just as my dad is being wheeled back down the hall after his shower. I follow behind.

As the nurses prepare to transfer him into the bed, he turns to me. "What were you doing at the nursing station?"

I know he'll be upset if he knew I spoke to the doctor about his condition. "I was asking where I could get a bottle of water."

He looks at me sideways, the same way he looked at me when he didn't believe me as a child. Thankfully, the issue is dropped when they lift him back into bed, and he's preoccupied by the pain.

Once Dad is settled, a man walks in, carrying a clipboard. "Would you like to sign up for a TV while you're here?" the man asks.

Dad brightens up. "How soon until it's delivered?"

The man laughs. "I'll put a rush on it."

"Just make sure you don't give him the channel that plays Jeopardy," I say quickly, "or you'll have to get earplugs for everyone else in the room."

Dad chuckles. "Smarten up."

Our visit lasts hours. Dad tells me stories about working up North with some of the Inuit, how they were tougher than the rest when enduring the sixty-below weather. Then the subject of his parents floats into the conversation—something he never spoke about when I was growing up. He mentions how his mother used to make a cherry pie that was so delicious, his mouth still waters at the memory. "Your mother was an excellent cook, but nothing could come close to my mom's cherry pie."

Of his father, he's brief. "He was a man of few words," he says, "Much like me."

I laugh. "Yeah, right!"

Every word my father speaks, I soak in and put away in the back of my mind. I know they will be all I have left of him someday soon.

It's well into the evening when my dad starts to yawn and the conversation fades. I stand up and touch his hand. He doesn't pull away this time. "I'll see you tomorrow. Okay?"

He smiles and his eyes flutter shut.

In the car, I grab my phone to look for messages. There are two: one from Ava, saying that she loves me and she'll see me at home later, and one from my boss, Don, sending well wishes for my father. I brush my thumb over Ava's message, re-reading the words.

It's 9PM. Ava will still be at her gig. Considering how I'm not as depressed as I expected to be over seeing my dad, I decide to surprise her by showing up for one of her sets.

It takes me about fifteen minutes to find The Bastion Street Lounge. It's busy, with no available parking in the front, so I drive around to the rear of the building and park before going in the back door.

The room is large. It's a lot bigger than the lounge in Ladysmith, and a lot busier too. I strain to see the stage, a long platform lit with red lights at the front of the room. Maneuvering through the people on my way to the bar, I scan the room for any sign of Ava. To the left of me is a foosball table and beyond that, in the corner, a small round table. I see the long, blonde hair—it's Ava, sitting at the table.

She's wearing a red shiny top and black leggings, and sitting with her is a man who has his back to me.

Using the crowd, I keep myself hidden as I watch the two talk, Ava leaning in close to hear him over the noise. My heart sinks, but I try to tell myself that the guy is probably just a fan—she's played a lot of places up and down the Island, and people know her.

Two women walk in front of me and block my view. I try to move around them without being spotted. Finally the duo moves, and I can see Ava and the man again.

Then, the guy pushes his chair back and stands up. He leans down and says something to Ava before grabbing his jacket off the back of the chair. His head is down as he walks toward the exit—toward me.

As he gets closer, he raises his head and all of the blood drains from my face.

It's him. It's the guy that was in my cab, and the same guy I saw Ava with at the gas station. I quickly turn my back as he walks past and out the exit door.

My mind is spinning and my heart is pounding, I'm so confused. *What the hell is going on here*?

I turn to see Ava walking toward the stage. This is the last place I want to be right now. I exit the building and get into my car, then just sit there, staring forward.

I'm totally blown away at what I just saw. She said she didn't know the man from the gas station. If that was true, why the hell was she sitting with him? Is she having an affair with the creepy looking guy?

Question after question pops into my mind, and I can't think of credible answers for any. There's only one thing I know for sure.

She is a liar.

Tears stream down my face the whole way home. Why did I let myself fall for this girl so hard? I thought she was different. I so badly wanted to spend the rest of my life with her. I'm such a fool.

By the time I pull up to the cabin, the hurt has been replaced by anger. All I can think of is gathering her belongings and setting them outside on the front step.

I don't want to talk to her. What would be the point in letting her try? She'd only lie again.

I slam the car door shut and stride into the cabin, shaking with rage.

In the bedroom, I open the dresser drawers and scoop up all her clothes, throwing them on the bed. Then I go into the closet and grab her large suitcase. I'm just about to close the closet doors when my eyes catch the small box on the upper shelf.

I stand on the tips of my toes and inch it toward me. I've almost got it in my grasp when it slides off the ledge and falls to the floor, spilling its contents everywhere.

Frustrated, I bend down and quickly gather pens, keychains, and magazines. Then I see the small journal. I pick it up and stare at it. I'm willing to bet she wrote all about her little affair in this book, and for a moment, I consider looking inside. It takes every bit of strength not to open it up but I know if I do, it will make me seem desperate and sneaky. Regardless of what she has done, I don't want to sink that low.

When I toss the journal into the box, small photos slide out through the bottom. I pick up the photos. The first is of two little girls standing in front of a swing set. One girl is blond, and the other has black hair. Flipping the picture over, I read the words *Jessica and Ava.*

I slide the picture underneath the others and look at the next one. There's a lady with blond hair and a man with dark hair sitting on the beach. Around them are three children. The girls I recognize as Jessica and Ava, but I have no idea who the other child is, and there's nothing written on the back. I flip to the last picture. This is of a man, and as soon as I see his face, I gasp. It's the guy from the lounge.

In the photo, he doesn't look as rugged and scary as he did in person. His eyes are warmer and the bone structure of his face is softer. I turn the picture over and see the words, *My brother, Cliff.*

A wave of relief washes through me, quickly followed by confusion.

Brother? The guy is her brother? She told me she had only one sibling. Jessica. Why would she lie about that? This is crazy.

I get up and go to the kitchen for a glass of water, then pace through the cabin, trying to make sense of everything.

I pull my phone from my pocket and see that it's a lot later than I thought. Ava will be home any minute. I quickly put her clothes back into the dresser, then return the suitcase and box to the closet, trying to make it look untouched.

As I wait on the couch, I don't know how I should be feeling. Ava did lie to me, but she didn't cheat. I guess I owe it to her to hear her out before I make any rash decisions.

Chapter Thirteen

The headlights cast a bright beam of yellow light through the window of the cabin. She's home.

I barely glance up when she walks in the door. "Hey, you're up," she says cheerfully, walking toward the couch.

I nod.

"How was your visit with your dad?"

"Fine."

"Is he feeling any better?" she says, dropping her bag on the sofa and placing her guitar on the floor.

"Yep."

She sits beside me. "Is something wrong?"

I look directly into her eyes. "When I was finished at the hospital, I stopped by the lounge to watch you play."

Her face pales and her eyes widen. She looks like she's seen a ghost. "Well, why didn't you say hi?" she says, trying to sound nonchalant. "Or signal to me that you were there?"

"You were busy."

"On stage?"

I shake my head. "Nope. You were busy talking to a man in the corner of the room. The same exact guy that was with you in the gas station parking lot. The guy that you said you didn't know."

She lowers her gaze to the floor. "I just…I just…"

"Who is the guy, Ava?"

"Nobody. He's nobody important."

Frustration boils up inside me. "You know what? Forget it." I hold up my hands. "I can't do this with you. I can't try and pull the truth out of you. I was in this relationship one hundred percent, full disclosure. And you, all you can do is lie. I can't do it. I won't do it. I want a solid relationship. Not one that's built on bullshit. I'm out."

She raises her head and looks at me. Tears are running down her face. "What are you saying? Are you telling me that the relationship is over?" Her voice crackles with emotion.

"What else am I supposed to do? You won't be straight with me. And if that's the case, then this relationship is like reading a story book. It's not real."

"Mila, you can't break up with me."

"You promised me, Ava. You promised that no matter how much you thought something would upset me, you'd tell me the truth. And then you just kept lying." I stand up. "All I know is that I'd rather feel alone by myself than feel alone when I'm with someone."

Ave grabs my arm. She's full-on sobbing now. "Okay. Okay. I'll tell you everything. The only reason I lied to you was to protect someone I love."

"What the hell does that mean?"

"Please, just sit back down and I'll explain."

"Fine." I sit. "But one more lie–"

"No more lies. I promise."

She shifts her body so she's looking directly into my eyes. "The man you saw me with in the parking lot of the gas station, I do know him. His name is Cliff. He's my older brother."

I exhale, relieved that she didn't give me yet another lie. "Why didn't you tell me you had a brother when we talked about siblings?"

"Because I was hoping he'd stay gone from our lives." There's a hard edge to her tone now. "He's a demented son of a bitch. He's been out East for a long time. Then, when Jessica was released from prison, he reared his ugly head. Even though we share the same parents, I don't consider him family. He's a career criminal and a chronic drug head."

"You think that Jessica tipped him off? About where you live?"

"I think she did, yes. She was always more…like-minded to his way of thinking and living."

"If you're not close to him, why are you speaking to him?"

Ava goes on to tell me about how Cliff has been trying to get money out of her for an outstanding debt he has with the wrong kind of people. "Gang members," she clarifies.

"But you don't owe him anything. If you feel nothing but contempt for him, can't you just tell him to piss off?"

"I tried, but he's desperate. He threatened me with something. A video on his cell phone."

"What's the video of?"

Ava takes a deep breath. "Jessica."

"Doing what?"

"She was lighting a fire. At a small cottage on the Nanaimo River."

"Do you mean one of the recent fires that happened?"

Ava nods.

"Okay." I reel with this information, but I try to look calm and collected for Ava's sake. "That's on Jessica. Not you. It doesn't give Cliff power to blackmail you."

"But it does, Mila."

"How?"

She gives me a look of anguish. "He knows me. And he knows how much I love Jess. If he shows the video to the cops, my sister will probably go to jail for the rest of her life. I wouldn't mind her doing some time for breaching her parole—hell, I'd welcome it, if only so she can get off dope and booze—but I would die inside if she had to spend the rest of her life behind bars." Tears well up in her eyes again.

I reach out and lay a hand briefly on hers. "I doubt they would give her life for starting another fire."

"Yes they would. If she lit a fire that killed a man."

"What do you mean?"

She stares at me silently, tears streaming from her eyes.

Then, it hits me. "Are you saying that the fire that killed someone was lit by your sister?"

She looks defeated. "I think so. I don't believe she would intentionally kill someone."

My chest constricts, making it hard to breathe. "This is bad, Ava. This is very bad."

"I know," she moans.

"And how much money is Cliff trying to blackmail you for?"

Ava wipes her eyes with the back of her hand. "He needs ten thousand dollars as soon as possible. I'm broke, and I've been racking my brain trying to figure out how to get him the cash, just so he'll go away. So far, I can't think of anything."

"Ava," I say softly. "There's a much bigger issue here than being blackmailed, or even your sister getting convicted. A man died."

She nods. "I know. I know he did. I keep feeding myself different lines of bullshit trying to make it okay."

"What could you possibly tell yourself to make it okay?"

"I don't know. I've been telling myself that if that man was still alive, a lot more people may have died from addiction and overdoses. I mean, he was in a drug lab when it burned down. Plus, he was probably an addict himself, and had family that were constantly worried about him. I'm not saying that I'm glad he's dead. I'm just saying that because he died, others may be better off." Her eyes are hard. I know she was thinking of her parents.

I put my hand on her leg. "I don't see it that way. I understand why you feel the way you do about drugs. I know how they devastated your family and ruined your childhood. But I look at it as a horrible disease. I think drug addiction affects the addict the most. Maybe if that man escaped the fire, he could've gotten well. Maybe even helped other addicts to get clean."

She nods slowly. "I guess I never thought of it that way. I only saw my own experience. When I think about what my sister and I were subjected to for years, all I can feel is resentment."

"It's okay, Ava. You have a right to your feelings, considering what you went through."

It's late, and we're both emotionally drained. I'm still not okay with Ava refusing to tell the cops what she knows, but right now my mind is too exhausted to think. She cuddles into me, and we fade off to sleep.

* * *

We spend the better part of the morning disinfecting my father's cabin, something the nurse at the hospital suggested. She told me that Dad needs to be in an environment that's as sterile as possible to help prevent infection in his weakened state. It's definitely a job we couldn't do if he was home, with all his inevitable bitching about me moving things around.

We head back to our cabin afterwards, where we continue avoiding talking about anything heavy, which suits me fine. I need to process everything about Cliff, the blackmail, and the fact Jessica could be responsible for a man's death.

"It's lunchtime," Ava says. "Do you want to grab a bite in town, or just make something here?"

"I was actually thinking of heading into Nanaimo to see Dad."

Ava looks immediately worried. "Do you think I could come along? I don't want to be alone right now."

"I don't think I should bring anyone to see Dad, Ava."

She nods quickly. "I completely understand. I just thought that while you're visiting with him, I could walk around the shops and maybe pick up some things."

As much as I feel the need to be alone on the way to Nanaimo, Ava looks nervous and I'd feel awful if I didn't agree to take her with me. "Okay, that sounds good."

* * *

"What the hell were you doing all morning?" Dad says when I walk into the room. "I've been waiting for you to come and take me out of this shit hole."

I laugh. "Well, you're obviously feeling like your normal self."

"Never mind, just get me out of here."

Knowing that my father won't be moved once he has his mind set on something, I tell him that I'll find out when his discharge day is.

At the nursing station, I ask if anyone one has spoken to my father about going home. A nurse flips through Dad's chart and tells me that he can go home tomorrow morning.

"Mila," my father yells from down the hall. "What the hell are you doing?"

I shake my head and give the nurse an apologetic smile. "Is the doctor still in the hospital?" I ask. "I'm just wondering if I could take Dad home today. He's starting to really protest being in the hospital, and trust me when I tell you that things will only amplify from here."

"I'll page the doctor and ask him." She hurries to the phone.

As I wait, my mind flashes on Ava. Her and my dad cannot be in the same car. If Dad does manage to get out of here today, I'll have to drive him home first, then hurry back to Nanaimo to pick Ava up.

Back in Dad's room, I tell him we have to wait to find out about leaving. This doesn't sit well with him. "I went through two wars for this country, and now some pissant doctor gets to decide about my freedom?" he hollers.

"Dad, you have literally never fought in a war. You were never even enlisted in the military."

"The doctor doesn't know that."

"Yelling isn't going to help you get out of here any faster."

Just then, the same nurse I was just speaking to walks in. "Mr. Dovey, I spoke with the doctor. We're going to get some prescriptions and a pill schedule together for you, and you'll be free to go home."

Expressionless, she turns on her heel and walks out.

Dad looks at me and grins. "Yelling isn't going to help me get out of here?"

"You're a real shit," I say, trying not to smile.

While Dad is changing into his street clothes with the help of a nurse, I wait in the hall and text Ava that my father is being released, and it'll be an hour or so before I can get her. Thankfully, she's not upset. She tells me that she's at the library, and for me to take my time.

* * *

So much has changed over the short time my dad was in the hospital. I want to tell him about Cliff, and how he's blackmailing Ava. Mostly though, I want to tell him—or anyone—about Jessica, and how she's likely responsible for a man's death.

But I can't. I can't say a word about any of it.

We stop at the Tasty Treat drive-thru and order two sundaes, then park down by the Departure Bay Terminal and watch the ferries come and go.

"Do you miss being in Vancouver?" he asks suddenly.

"I did at first," I say honestly. "But not now."

"Not now that you've discovered what a charming dad you have?"

"Yeah, that's it. You nailed it."

"Lies!" He winks. He's quiet for a few moments. "This Ava bird. You like her a lot, huh?"

Shocked that he's asking about my relationship, I look at him closely to make sure he's being serious. I don't want to answer if he's baiting me for a debate. "I do, Dad. I love her."

"Love? That's a strong word."

"It's a strong emotion. I never planned on falling for her, it just kind of happened."

"Well, that's how it goes. Love kind of picks us. We don't choose who we'll be connected to."

I nod, still shocked that he is talking to me about it.

"Should we go?" I say, taking his empty sundae cup from him and setting it on the floor.

"Yes. I'm starting to feel a little tired. Listen, I know you have things to do, but I need to sit and talk to you about something after I have a nap and you do whatever it is you need to do today."

"Talk to me about what?"

"Just drive. You ask too many damn questions."

* * *

On my way back to downtown Nanaimo, I stop at a grocery store and pick up a few ingredients.

As soon as I arrive at the library, I see Ava standing at the entrance. I'm pulling up to the doors when I see an elderly woman drop her bag of books. I watch as Ava hurries over and helps the woman repack her bag.

I wonder how I could've been so ready to break up with someone so selfless and caring. One whiff of something suspicious, and I jumped right to the worst-case scenario. Her heartbroken face when I said I wanted to end things flashes in my memory. I was so wrong.

No matter what happens between us, I can never give up on her again. No matter what baggage she brings to our relationship, she's worth it.

Ava spots my car, waves, and makes her way over to me. Once in the car, she pulls a book out of her bag. "I thought we could read this together sometime," she says, showing me the cover. *Toxic Family, Toxic Life.*

I smile. "I guess that title relates to both of our families."

When we get home, Ava helps me carry the groceries inside. She pulls out a can of cherries from the bag. "What are these for?"

I grin at her. "I was wondering if you wanted to help me make a cherry pie for my father."

I tell her his story about how his mother would make the best cherry pies. Ava goes on her laptop and looks up old-fashioned pie recipes while I get all the ingredients out and arrange them on the counter. I'm a bit nervous. I've never attempted to make a crust before, and Ava can't cook to save her life, so we'll be winging it.

"Okay, I think I found the perfect recipe," Ava says, looking up from her laptop. "Did you buy a ready-made crust?"

"Nope. I thought we'd just figure it out."

"Really?" she says skeptically.

I laugh. "Where's your sense of adventure?"

"It's definitely not with baking."

"Let's just do it. Read me what we need for the crust."

She reads me the ingredients and their measurements. I add everything to the bowl and use my hands to mix it. Instantly, I can tell something is off. The mixture is really mucky.

Ava walks over and peers into the bowl. "That doesn't look like the picture," she says. "Maybe we should add more flour?"

She takes a cup of flour and dumps it into the bowl while I keep working the dough. Soon, it starts to firm up.

"What do you think?" I ask. "Does it look better now?"

"It reminds me of playdough. I think we should add more water."

She dumps more water in the bowl and it becomes too wet. Again, she adds flour until it's too dry. By the time we've repeated these steps a few more times, my hands are aching and I'm starting to sweat. "Okay I can't mix this mess anymore." I lift my dough-covered hands from the dough and flex my fingers. "I'm going to get arthritis. Let's just try to roll it out with a bottle."

Ava sprinkles flour on the counter. I take the heavy hunk of dried clay out of the bowl and drop it with a thud on the counter. We press the ball down as much as we can, then take turns trying to roll it out.

"It's not spreading very well, is it?" Ava says.

By the time we're done, there's flour and pieces of hard dough everywhere. We try to push the dough into the baking dish, but it keeps cracking and falling apart. By the time we've added the canned cherries and the top layer of hard dough, it looks more like a patchwork quilt than a pie. We both stare at it and laugh before putting it in the oven.

"It's the thought that counts, right?" asks Ava, still laughing.

"I hope Dad sees it that way."

While our awful abomination bakes, Ava has a shower and gets ready for another night at the lounge. Meanwhile, I tackle the crusty dishes and dough-covered kitchen.

"Are you coming to watch me play?" she asks, tuning her guitar.

"I don't know." I wipe up some of the flour from the counter and dump it in the sink. "Unless you're worried about your brother showing up, I should probably stay home so I can check on Dad."

"I don't think Cliff will show again so soon. He said he'd be in touch in a couple of days."

"You're not actually considering paying him, are you?"

"I don't know if I have a choice. He wants ten grand, which I obviously don't have."

"What are you going to do?"

"I have no idea." She rests her chin on her guitar, looking morose. "I could sell my car. I might get half of what he's asking me for."

"You can't sell your car, you need it."

"I'm aware of that, Mila. But if it made him disappear, it would be worth it."

The oven timer goes off. I grab a tea towel, open the oven door, and pull out the makeshift pie. I place it on the counter.

The top looks like a crime scene. Blood red sauce bubbles out of every crack and hole. Despite its gruesome appearance, it actually smells pretty good.

"Maybe you can blindfold him as he eats," Ava says, looking at the pie.

"Would you eat it?"

"I'd have to be pretty hungry, and I certainly wouldn't pay for it."

Ava soon leaves for her gig, and I finish cleaning up the kitchen while I wait for the pie to cool. As much as I miss Ava when we're apart, I'm looking forward to some alone time after I get back from Dad's.

When the pie is cool enough to handle, I take it next door.

As soon as I walk in, Dad zeros in on what I'm carrying. "What did you bring me, shit on a shingle?"

You don't know how close you are, Dad. "I remembered what you told me about your mom's cherry pies, so I thought I'd give it a shot."

He looks taken aback. "You went to all of that trouble for me?"

"Don't get too excited until you taste it. We had a bit of trouble with the crust."

"Crusts are a tricky thing. It may take a knack."

"Well, this one may take a chainsaw to cut."

"Get some plates. I'm up for the challenge."

I put the pie on the counter and grab the sharpest looking knife from the drawer. Thankfully, the TV is on, so Dad can't hear the sawing sounds as I carve into the pie.

With two pieces on saucers, I grab a couple of forks and sit next to Dad on the couch. "I hope you have good dental insurance," I say, handing him the pie. "Proceed with caution."

He taps the dense crust with his fork. A small chunk gives way. He scoops up the nickel-size morsel and puts it in his mouth. Almost immediately, he glares at me. "What do you call this? Revenge pie?"

"Very funny. Just don't eat it."

"No. No. You made it for me, so I'm going to eat it." He pushes down hard with his fork and tries to eat another chunk of the crust. He spits it out, then looks at the small piece intently.

"What's wrong?"

"For a moment, I thought I'd eaten a piece of the plate."

"Okay, that's it. Give me that damn thing." I take our saucers and place them on the counter.

He snickers. "Aw, you're not going to eat yours?"

"I'm saving mine for later."

"Don't dump it into the bin. As much as I'm not a fan of pesky raccoons, I'd feel terrible if one of them unfortunate buggers got into the garbage and tried to bite that crust."

We watch a Carol Burnett rerun and laugh our asses off. Thankfully, Dad hasn't needed to take one of his pain pills since I've been here. His face looks relaxed and stress-free, like it did before I took him to emergency the other day.

Ava texts me right before she goes on stage to play her first set. *How did the pie taste?*

I text back, saying that it was definitely not a success, and the pie confirms that neither she nor I are bakers.

I put my phone down and sigh. Then I remember something, and I turn to Dad. "Dad, you said earlier today that there was something you wanted to talk to me about."

He asks me to get him a drink of water. "I need to get the taste of papier-mache out of my mouth."

When he has his water and has gargled and swallowed a few times, he sets the glass down and turns to me. "I wanted to discuss money with you."

"Money? Why? Do you need a few bucks? I don't have much, but you're welcome to—"

"No, dammit," he interrupts. "Just close your yap and listen to me for a minute."

"Okay. I'm sorry. Finish what you were going to say."

"When I die—"

"Dad, I don't want to hear this—"

"Are you going to sit there and shut up, or do I have to gag you?"

I sigh. "Fine."

"As I was trying to say, I want to talk to you about when I die. You need to know this, so pay attention! I have a few bucks in my bank account for you. And you're going to

194

need to have your head on straight when you figure out how to spend it."

"Why? How much is there?"

He shrugs. "About seventy-five thousand by now."

I roll my eyes. "You're hilarious."

"That's what is there, Mila. And I don't want you blowing it on stupid shit. Put it toward something like an apartment or a new car or something. Don't just piss it away."

I study his face, trying to see the joke. He looks dead serious. "Dad, I'm confused. Are you saying you have seventy-five thousand bucks and you've been living like a pauper?"

"I live just fine. I have everything I need."

"Are you kidding? Look at this couch we're sitting on—it has bigger humps than a camel. Not to mention the rickety card table you eat at. I'm surprised it hasn't fallen off its legs yet."

"It has. I fixed it. And as for the couch, why would I go out and replace something that works perfectly fine for me?"

I'm trying to think of something else to say, but I'm in such shock, I can't think of anything. My mom used to say that Dad was so cheap, he'd haggle with the paperboy. She'd tell me about going shopping, and when the store charged a nickel for a bag, Dad would balance the groceries in his arms and carry them to the car.

"I don't want your money," I finally say.

"Don't be stupid. What the hell am I supposed to do with it? There're no shopping malls in heaven."

"Heaven? Are you sure you've got that right?" I say, trying to lighten the dark conversation.

"Very funny." He smirks. "Anyway, I want you to think long and hard about something practical to do with the money."

"Did Mom know you had a whole bunch of cash stuffed away?"

"Of course she did. Some of it was hers. We were saving it for you."

I feel like crying. He was such a gruff asshole for most of my childhood. It doesn't surprise me that Mom would think ahead and save money for me, but I never dreamt my father would. He was always an "every man for himself" kind of guy…or so I thought.

"I feel overwhelmed, Dad. I don't know what to say."

"Say nothing. Especially if it's going to be emotional and long-winded."

I laugh. "Gee, Dad, I should send those words into Hallmark. You'd make a fortune."

"Smartass. You feel like having a pizza? I do. Call for one. And considering your new-found wealth, you're buying."

* * *

My bed is a comforting sight after a long day.

196

As soon as I lie back, my head melts into the pillow. Thoughts of my father swirl through my mind. I've never been financially motivated, which is a trait of mine that always spawned debate with him. But the fact that he'd been socking away all that cash to make sure I'd be okay when he died changes everything I thought I knew about his character.

He's the rudest, grumpiest codger I've ever met. But underneath that prickly exterior lies a heart. Mom always said he had one, but I thought she was just seeing him through rose-colored glasses.

Chapter Fourteen

I wake with sunlight pooling into the room. The first thing I do is stretch an arm out and feel for Ava beside me—she's here. It's unusual for me to sleep for so long, and so deeply, especially since Ava wasn't home when I went to bed. I didn't even hear her come in last night. Quietly, I get out of bed and stumble to the kitchen to make some coffee.

It's not long before Ava wakes as well. I'm sitting on the couch drinking my coffee when she comes out of the bedroom and sits next to me, snuggling against my side, still warm from being in bed. I relax into her, and for a while we sit quietly, enjoying each other's company.

At one point, Ava asks about my father. In a flash, I remember the conversation from last night's visit. The money my dad has saved for me.

I open my mouth to tell Ava, but after a moment, I decide against it. It's a big conversation, and I don't feel like discussing money right now. I just want a relaxing morning with the girl I love. "It was great," I say simply, resting my chin on the top of her head.

After I finish my coffee, I head to the bathroom and shower. I'm in a good mood this morning, and I hum as I dry off. It's only when I throw a soap wrapper in the bin and see something else inside that my mood clouds. Inside the bin is an empty pill bottle, and with a frown I fish it out.

It's the same bottle I had found a while ago. *Olanzapine*. I'd wanted to ask Ava about the prescription the last time I saw it, but we weren't close enough for me to delve into her personal life back then. Plus, I thought she'd eventually tell me, but she never did.

Seeing the bottle again now, I feel a stronger desire to know what the medication is for. After recent events, I feel strongly that there shouldn't be any secrets between us.

A small voice in my head reminds me how I haven't mentioned the money that my father is leaving me, either. I don't know why. I just haven't.

I will. Eventually. It just doesn't feel like the right time. And it's not like I even have the money yet.

I pull on my robe, then grab the bottle from the counter and head for the door. Before I can leave, Ava walks in. "Hey, beautiful," she says, smiling and wrapping her arms around my waist. She kisses me softly.

I pull back, and she looks confused. I hold up the empty bottle in my hand, and her eyes lock onto it. "Ava," I say. "I found this in the trash. What's the prescription for?"

She seems put on the spot and doesn't answer for a few seconds. "Oh," she blurts out, "it's nothing really. It's just to help me sleep. They're very mild."

"Why didn't you tell me before?"

She takes the bottle and tosses it in the trash. "Because, silly, I didn't think of it. I only take them when I get really bad insomnia. It's no big deal." She reaches into the shower and turns the water back on. "Now, can we stop talking about that, and get on to more important things? Like what you want to do tomorrow for fun? Tonight is my last night at the lounge, so we can do whatever we want." She kisses me once more, then disrobes and hops into the shower.

Over the day, Ava spends hours going over original songs and cover tunes that she's planning on adding to her setlist. I do some cleaning and give Dad a call—he seems fine, which is a relief. All the talk about death last night put worries in my brain.

Later, as evening approaches, Ava dresses for work in a black mini-dress and open toed mules, and slicks her hair back in a tight ponytail. Looking at this woman I'm with, I'm amazed all over again.

"Are you going to swing by tonight?" she asks, applying a glossy red stain to her lips.

"I could. Dad seemed fine on the phone. He said there wasn't really a point for me to pop by."

"Ok, then. I guess I'll see you later." She kisses me goodbye and heads out.

Once I'm alone, I hurry into the bedroom and tear through my clothes. I don't want to go in the same predictable jeans and a t-shirt. I'd like for Ava to see me the way I see her—sexy.

It takes fifteen minutes of sorting through my things before I realize that I desperately need to invest in a new wardrobe. Reluctantly, I settle on my nicest pair of jeans and my Ozzy t-shirt.

Once I'm dressed, I go into the bathroom and use Ava's curling iron to style my hair, something I never do. After struggling with the iron for fifteen minutes, I grab her hairspray, give my head a few squirts, and spend the next five minutes coughing and hacking from the aerosol fumes. For the finishing touch, I go through the bathroom drawer and find a light pink lipstick, which I carefully apply with an uncertain hand.

I stare at the final result in the mirror, second guessing every choice I made. I never go out looking so dolled-up. I feel awkward and a bit embarrassed, but I remind myself that this is for Ava. I just hope she appreciates it.

* * *

The sound of Ava's singing comes through the lounge door as I grab the handle. As soon as I walk inside, I see a packed room and Ava on the stage. I'm struck with amazement at the sheer number of people watching my girlfriend perform. I maneuver my way through the back of the room and up to the bar, where I sit on a stool and turn toward the stage in hopes she sees me amongst the crowd.

After each tune, she engages the audience, asking people where they're from and taking the odd song request. I look out over the crowd; I can tell by the focus and smiles on the faces that they love her.

When her first set is over, she walks right up to the bar to where I'm sitting. I feel a flash of pride as she sits next to me, beaming. "You look stunning," she says.

"Really?"

"Oh yeah." She touches a strand of my curled hair. "Did you do all this for me?"

"Maybe." I laugh, feeling embarrassed.

Just then, a dark-haired, athletic guy walks up. "Hey, ladies, can we buy you a drink?" He motions to a table, where another man of equal good looks is sitting.

Ava and I glance at each other. She winks at me, then tells the guy that she has to go back up on stage now.

The man nods, then zeros in on me. "Do you want to join us?"

"No. I'm fine here, thanks."

When he walks away, Ava and I laugh.

"Are you going to stick around for a while?" Ava asks me.

"I don't think so. I wouldn't want Rico Suave to come back over here." I've never been one to stay for too long in a bar. It's just not my thing.

Thankfully, Ava understands and doesn't take offence. "I don't blame you. I'm lucky—I have the stage to separate myself from everyone else."

"I'll be at home," I say, getting up. I want to kiss her, but I'm not sure how that would affect her popularity, so I just gently touch her on the arm.

"See you later, then," she says before turning and walking toward the stage.

* * *

A loud thump wakes me, and I immediately sit up on the couch.

I look around the room, then stand up and look out the windows into the dark night. I can't see a thing. I grab my phone and look at the time—it's after midnight, Ava should be home by now.

Looking through the door window, I see her car parked in front of the cabin. I check the bedroom, but she's not there. She must've just gotten home. I slide on my shoes and put on my jacket so I can go outside and help with her things.

I open the front door, and immediately I see Ava on the top step, slumped over.

"Ava? Why are you just sitting there? What's wrong?"

She doesn't answer. I kneel down and lift her chin, but I can barely see her in the darkness. Then, she lets out a weak moan.

"Ava, did you fall? Are you okay?"

She mumbles something inaudible then slumps her head forward again.

My heart is pounding hard. I'm hyperventilating when I race into the cabin to grab my phone.

Back on the stoop, I turn on my phone light and shine it on her. She's a mess. Her face is covered in blood and there's a large open cut on her forehead with wisps of her blond hair stuck to it.

"Ava! What the hell happened to you?" I can feel tears rolling down my cheeks.

When she doesn't answer, I maneuver my way behind her and grab under her arms. I pull her inside and lay her on the floor, then sprint to the bedroom to grab a pillow, stopping at the sink on my way through the kitchen to grab a wet paper towel.

I ease the pillow under her head and gently begin to wipe the blood from her face. Tears continue streaming down my face, but I work to keep my voice calm. "Ava, I'm going to call the ambulance, okay?"

"No," she moans. "You can't."

Despite my relief at her finally talking to me, I hold firm. "You're hurt, and I can't tell how badly. You need to be checked out."

"Do not call anyone." Her voice is a little stronger.

"What happened? Did you bang your head? Did you fall or faint or something?"

"No. It was him. He did this to me."

"Someone did this to you? Who?"

"Cliff," she says, slightly opening her eyes.

"Your brother?"

"Yes."

All of a sudden it's clear to me why she won't let me call for help. Despite every instinct telling me to, I hold off on calling the ambulance.

After about fifteen minutes of me slowly wiping the blood from her face, she gains more clarity, and her words are clearer.

She left the lounge at the end of the night and had driven all the way home without incident. However, when she got out of the car, someone grabbed her by the back of the neck. She managed to turn around and see Cliff towering over her. "His eyes were crazy. He kept asking for his money, then said that if I didn't pay him right away, he was going to kill me. I tried to reason with him, but anything I said only made him angrier.

"When he finally let go of me, I tried to make it to the door, but he started punching me in the back of the head. I turned to face him, and that's when he did this to my face. Things went black after that."

I feel sick with guilt. I was asleep on the couch just feet away from where Ava was being attacked, and I had no idea. Why couldn't I have woken up just a few minutes earlier? "I'm so sorry, Ava. I was trying to wait up for you, but I dozed off."

"It's not your fault, sweetie," she says softly, reaching up and brushing the tears from my cheeks. "I feel awful that this happened here. If I was a better person, I would never have dragged you into my life."

"No, Ava–"

"In the short time I've known you, you've had to put up with my crazy sister and my psycho brother." She takes a shuddering breath. "I knew there was a possibility of my siblings showing up to ruin my life—they've done it before—but I should never have pulled you into it. The thing is, I never counted on loving you so much." Tears spill from her eyes.

I cradle her face gingerly, careful not to hurt her. "I love you, too. And don't be silly—your siblings have nothing to do with you and me. You're not them. I don't blame you for any of it and I don't regret a thing. I just want to get past all of this so we can live our lives in peace. Together."

Ava gives me a weak, teary smile, then asks me to help her sit up. I do, feeling a new wave of anxiety at just how weak she seems. After a few minutes, she manages to stay upright on her own, bracing herself with her hands on the floor. "Can you get me some water," she asks, and I comply.

Worried she has a concussion, I look up signs and symptoms and ask her a series of questions. So far, she isn't nauseous, and she is able to focus, so I feel a small amount of relief. Still, it's hard for me not to worry as I watch her make her way to the couch at a painfully slow pace, wincing with every movement.

Repeatedly, I beg that she let me take her to the hospital, but she's adamant about not going. So I make her a cup of tea, which she takes about five sips of before shuffling to bed, steadying herself on my arm.

It's a long night for me as I watch her sleep, making sure she's okay after being hit in the head. All I can think about is my hatred for Cliff, and how he needs to pay for what he's done.

* * *

The morning dew glistens in the early sun as I look blearily out the window. I'm waiting for Ava to finish in the bathroom. She's in the shower, washing the dried blood from her hair and face. She looks a mess with cuts across the bridge of her nose and her forehead, but thankfully, the dizziness is gone.

As we eat a light breakfast, she tells me that she has to go into town to refill her prescription. I demand to go with her, in case her psycho brother is lurking around.

After we're dressed and Ava has done a pretty effective job covering her war wounds with makeup, we head to the drugstore. I wait in the car when she goes into the pharmacy, but I keep an eye on the door, ready to jump out at any sign of Cliff following her inside.

Through the windshield, I watch as a guy in his twenties helps an old man walk down the street. A grandfather and grandson, I'm guessing. As I watch them, something occurs to me. How can I go to work and leave Ava alone at the cabin? What if her brother shows up again? And what about my father? He's just next door. He's in danger, too.

I can't help blaming Jessica for telling Cliff where we live. Now, not only do I have to worry about Ava's safety, but also my sick father's wellbeing.

The only logical solution is to quit my job. At least for now.

Ava walks out of the store and gets in the car. "Sorry for taking so long. The pharmacist had to call my doctor in Victoria to have my prescription verified."

On the way home, I stop at the cab stand. "I just need to have a quick word with Don," I tell Ava, undoing my seatbelt. "I'll be right back."

Don isn't in the office, but there's a lady receptionist sitting at his desk, answering the phone and typing on the computer. I wait until she's no longer busy, then tell her that I need to leave a message for Don. She types out my resignation and sends it to him.

I walk back to my car, feeling horrible about walking out on my job without giving much notice. But what else can I do?

We stop at a market and buy groceries for dinner. Once we're home, Ava takes the bags inside and I go next door to check on Dad.

He's sitting at his table, poking at a couple of eggs and some toast on a plate in front of him. As soon as I see him, I want to tell him about what happened to Ava last night, and how I just quit my job…but I can't. He's sick and doesn't need to be burdened by any of my bad news. The least I can do is to try to be upbeat, no matter how messed up I'm feeling.

"Is that supposed to be your lunch, Dad?"

"No. It was my breakfast that they dropped off hours ago. I was going to eat the lunch meal until I got a look at it."

"Why? It couldn't have been worse than cold eggs and soggy toast."

"Well, it was. As soon as I lifted the lid, I saw thick yellow sludge. I think it was supposed to be a cream of squash soup, but it looked more like baby shit."

I shake my head. "Gross, Dad. And how would you know what baby shit looks like? Something tells me you weren't the diaper-changing type."

"On that you're right, but I always seemed to walk in the room when your mom was changing you. It made me gag every time. You should be ashamed of yourself."

I laugh. "I am. Throughout my whole life, I've felt guilty about you having to see my dirty diapers."

Over the next hour, we watch TV and I make sure he has everything he needs until I come back tomorrow. He informs me that the mobile lab people are coming by to take his blood and run a few more tests tomorrow. He also tells me that an old pal he and Mom used to play cards with is stopping by in the afternoon. I tell Dad that I'll pick up dinner tomorrow night and we can spend the evening together.

* * *

I'm just about to turn the handle and walk into my cabin when I notice a smudge of dried blood high up on the door. It stops me for a minute. When I found Ava last night, she was slumped over on the top step. I assumed Cliff punched her and knocked her out cold before she reached the door. I guess I was wrong. I feel a fresh wave of guilt, imagining Ava trying to get through the door, and me sleeping through it completely.

For the remainder of the day, Ava and I stay close. I fuss over her, putting ointment on her wounds and brushing her hair. She tells me how grateful she is that we found one another.

We're about halfway through dinner when I bring up the money my father saved for me. Ava stops eating and stares at me. "You're kidding. Your dad has seventy-five grand saved for you?"

"Yeah, something like that."

"That's incredible. What are you going to do with it?"

"To be honest, I haven't really thought about it much."

Ava looks at me in disbelief. "If I knew I had that much money waiting for me, I wouldn't stop thinking about it."

I laugh. "I don't know. I guess I've never really been a money person. If I have enough cash to get by, that's good enough for me."

"I can't believe you're saying that. I mean…you could really change your life with seventy-five grand."

"Why would I want to change my life? I've got you."

Ava reaches over and brushes my face with the back of her hand. "You're so sweet and you're definitely different from anyone else I've been with. The type of girls I've dated in the past were all about money and taking what they could from me."

"That's horrible, Ava."

She smiles. "Yeah, but it doesn't matter now, that's all behind me."

Later on, while lying beside her in bed, I feel happy about mentioning the money. Finally, there are no secrets between us.

* * *

We wake to the sound of rain beating against the cabin windows. Ava rolls over and looks at me. I gently move the strands of hair from her face. Her injuries are healing nicely. I gently kiss around the wounds before pressing my lips against hers.

After some time lying together and waking up, Ava tells me that she plans on working on songs all day. I mention my plans to have dinner next door with Dad. "Will you be nervous staying home alone?" I ask.

"I'm not worried. I know Cliff—he won't come back here for a while. He's waiting for me to raise the money and call him. He thinks I'm scared because of what he did to me the other night, but I'm not. My fear of him has turned to anger, and if he ever tries to hurt me again, I'll fight back."

"But you're still planning on paying him?"

Ava nods. "I don't see any other choice. I know him. He doesn't bluff. If I don't come through, he'll turn the video into the police and Jess will be locked in prison forever. But if I can raise the money, he'll pay his debts and leave."

"But, Ava...even if you do give him the money, what's stopping him from doing this again? How do you know he won't turn up years from now with a new demand, and threaten to use the video against her again?"

"He said he'll erase the video."

"And you believe him?"

"No, not even a little bit. But what I'm counting on is him going back East after he pays whatever hoodlums he owes money to. He's probably burned his bridges here, so he'll likely want to get the hell away as soon as he can. I think that's why he hurt me in the first place. He's desperate. Someone is probably putting the screws to him."

"Have you given any more thought to how you'll pay him?"

"The only idea I've come up with is selling my car. That gets me half of the ten grand he's asking for. As for the other half..."

She sighs and picks at the pillowcase. "I don't know how I'll raise that kind of cash."

"Well, maybe I can help. I probably have a couple thousand in my accounts, but I'd have to check."

"No, sweetie. I don't want to take money from you and leave you short."

"We're together. Whatever problems arise, we deal with as a team."

* * *

The beautiful sounds of her music drift from the cabin behind me as I walk next door. Despite Ava's confidence, I'm nervous as hell leaving her alone. But Ava promised to send me texts throughout the evening to let me know she's okay. Plus, I didn't leave until I made sure every window and door was locked tightly.

Dad's face is ashen and drawn when he answers the door.

"Dad. How are you feeling?"

"I've had a long day dealing with those lab techs," he says, heading back to the sofa. "And the visit with my old pal went longer than expected."

"Did you want to reschedule our dinner plans so you can rest?"

"Shut up and order us a pizza."

I scroll through the channels while we wait for our food. There's nothing on but news, a nature show, and the movie *On*

Golden Pond, which I saw with Mom over a decade ago. I settle on the movie. Dad watches the screen for a couple of minutes, then says, "I hope to hell this isn't a girl movie."

"Dad, it's barely started. Give it a chance. The lead character is a cantankerous old man just like you, you may like it."

Over the next half hour, Dad gets quieter. At one point, he reaches for his pills.

"Is the pain bad right now?" I ask.

"I'm fine. Watch your damn girl movie." He pops a couple of tablets into his mouth.

A few moments later, the pizza guy arrives. After I pay, I put a couple of pieces of pizza on saucers and rejoin Dad on the couch. "Did I miss anything?"

"No, but I wish I did."

"You seriously don't like the movie?"

"It's fine for a melodrama."

I shake my head and smile.

I finish a few more slices, then glance over at Dad's plate and notice he hasn't touched his food. "Don't you like your pizza? Did you want me to make you something else? You've got to eat."

He looks at me and rolls his eyes. "Yes, Mother, I know. I'll eat as soon as my pills kick in."

The movie is two-thirds finished when I see him start to nibble on his pizza, signifying that the medication has started to take effect and his pain has eased. I breathe a sigh of relief.

When the show ends, Dad shuts off the TV, something he never does.

"Did you want to go to sleep now?" I start to stand. "I can leave if you want."

"No. Don't leave. I just wanted to talk to you without distraction from the boob-tube."

"Okay, what do you want to talk about?"

"Nothing too pressing. I just thought that if you weren't busy tomorrow morning, we could take a drive to the old house we lived in when your mom was still alive. What do you think about that?"

My father isn't much of a sentimental person, so I'm a bit surprised at his request. "If you like, sure. We can go there. It'll be strange seeing the house after all these years. I haven't been back there since Mom died."

"Nor me."

"Why now? Why, after all this time, do you want to go back there?"

"I've been thinking about your mom a lot lately. More than usual, and I'm not sure why. Maybe if I see the old place, it'll slow my mind down a bit."

I nod. "I understand. I'll be here early and we'll take a drive out there. Maybe we can grab some brunch afterwards."

"I'd like that," he says, clicking the TV back on. "I'm starting to feel tired now. Maybe I should try to get some sleep."

I gather our plates and rinse them while Dad watches TV. I've just put the leftover pizza in the fridge when he says abruptly, "That girlfriend of yours and her wing-nut sister–"

"What about them?" I interrupt.

"I don't trust them. I want you to watch your ass."

I chuckle. "Dad, you've literally said the same thing about every friend I've introduced you to when I was growing up."

"Yeah. I'm sure I did. You were never that good at sizing people up."

"I beg to differ," I say, but pause. He has a point. "I agree with you about Jessica, Ava's sister. She's a real piece of work. But she's gone now. It's just Ava and me at the cabin."

"Ava is related to Jessica. One bad seed affects the whole tree."

"Interesting perspective." I smirk, not wanting the discussion to continue.

When I've got my shoes and jacket on and am getting ready to open the door, my father calls out one more time. "Thanks for the pizza," he says. "You're the best daughter I've ever had. Notwithstanding, you're my only child."

I'm overjoyed at the sentiment, but can't help thinking, *those must be good pills!*

* * *

Ava is lying on the bed, writing in her journal when I walk in. When she looks up and smiles, a warm feeling rushes through me. Even with her wounds, she's still strikingly beautiful.

We talk for a while. I tell her how much I'm looking forward to going to the old house with Dad tomorrow, then we have a long shower together before calling it a night.

* * *

Sipping my coffee, I stand at the window and look out over the glistening water. It's a beautiful morning—perfect weather for my outing with Dad.

Ava walks up behind me and wraps her arms around my waist. She softly kisses my shoulders and neck, sending chills up my spine. I turn around and press my lips against hers, then whisper, "We'll finish this later."

She smiles, then walks over to the couch and sits down as I get ready to leave. "You know what, Mila?" she says, watching me. "I think we're going to have a wonderful life together. Maybe one day we could move to a place with a garden, and maybe even a music room. I think that's my dream. To be with you, some place quiet, away from people and noise. Just the two of us in our private little bubble."

I walk over to kiss her goodbye. "That's a great dream. I think that will be mine, too."

* * *

The TV is on, and Dad is curled up on the couch. His eyes are closed and he looks peaceful.

I hate to wake him, but we've got a big morning planned and he still has to get up, eat and get dressed.

I nudge him then stand back. He's never been a morning person and when he gets woken up, he can be quite reactive. He doesn't budge. "Come on, sleepy head, wake up."

He's usually a light sleeper, but maybe the pills the doctor gave him really knock him out. Hopefully, he didn't take a double dose by mistake. I lean over him and shake his shoulder. "Dad, wake up! You're scaring me."

There's still no response.

With the back of my hand, I feel his face. It's cold—really cold.

I kneel down in front of the couch, my face just inches from his. "Dad? Please be okay. Please wake up," I whisper. But inside, I know that he's already gone. I feel it.

I rest my head on his shoulder. "I don't want you to go, not now." A sob rips from my chest. "I'm not done loving you yet. I need you so much. I wanted to tell you how much

I loved you, and always have." I put my arm around his emaciated body. "I hope you have a peaceful journey, Dad. If you see Mom, please tell her how much I love her and that I miss her every day."

Dad's shirt is soaked from my tears. Heartbroken and overwhelmed with pain, I sit back, grab one of his hands and look at him for a long while.

Eventually, I slide my phone out of my pocket and make the call.

Chapter Fifteen

"Mila." Ava sits on the bed. "Please get up. You've been in bed for four days, and I'm really starting to worry."

It takes a moment to muster the energy to answer. "I just want to sleep a while longer."

"That's all you've been saying. You've got to get up and eat something. This isn't healthy."

"What do you want from me?" I'm unable to keep the resentful tone out of my voice.

"I want you to make an effort. That's all I'm asking. And if you won't try for yourself, try for me."

"I will, okay? But right now, I just want to be left alone. I'm so tired."

Ava crawls in beside me and presses her body against my back. "Okay, fine. If you won't get up, I'll lie here with you and we can both starve and stink. And believe me, Mila, you are really starting to ripen."

"I don't care."

Ava sighs.

"I'm an orphan, Ava."

"So am I. But you're alive and you have your life ahead of you. You can be sad, Mila, you're supposed to be. But you still have to take care of yourself. Your father wouldn't have wanted you to give up."

"I know. Just let me sleep for a little while longer and I'll get up."

"And you'll eat something?"

"Yes, Ava. I promise." I pull the blanket over my head.

* * *

A giant wave of icy water rushes over my skin, causing me to lose my breath. I sit up to see Ava holding an empty pail.

"Have you lost your damn mind?" I yell.

"Are you mad, Mila?"

"What do you think?"

"Good! Coffee is ready and your breakfast is on the table." She turns and walks out of the room.

"You're the devil," I say, slowly getting out of the soaked bed. My legs feel weak and wobbly.

After changing out of my wet clothes into my robe, I walk out and sit at the table. "That wasn't a very nice thing you did."

"Yeah, well, I love you, and everything else I tried didn't work."

I slowly get through a piece of toast and a couple spoonfuls of porridge. Ava hands me a cup of coffee.

"What should we do today?" she asks. "After you shower."

"I've already had one. An icy cold, unwelcome one."

Ava smiles. "If you don't go into that bathroom and shower once you've finished your coffee, what I did in the bedroom will seem minor compared to what else I have up my sleeve."

"I don't want to be pushed like this. I'm grieving, Ava. My father just died."

"Yep, he sure did and that's an awful thing. But it doesn't give you the right to give up. I think we should go for a nice walk on the beach together."

I look out of the window. I hadn't even noticed the sun shining outside.

* * *

The sea breeze feels cleansing as it pushes against us while we stroll hand-in-hand on the beach. Squawking gulls swoop down to scavenge for food at the water's edge, then take flight as we approach. My head feels heavy and my heart aches, but the longer we walk, the clearer my mind becomes.

We sit on a log about a mile up the beach. Ava sings me a new song she's been working on, and the pain I have inside starts to ease.

* * *

It's been a busy three weeks dealing with the aftermath of my father's death. Ava and I cleaned out his cabin, keeping only a few mementos that remind me of him; pictures of him and Mom that he had on his wall, letters that she wrote him when he was away working, and his shotgun that he loved so much.

I also gained access to his accounts, paid off any remaining debts he had and deposited the remaining money, including the seventy-five grand, into my accounts.

Ava has been my rock through everything, helping me when I've needed it and talking me through the sad spells. Tonight, I'm going to surprise her with a thank you gift: dinner at a seafood restaurant and a movie. After what she's done for me, she deserves a night out.

* * *

She steps out of the bedroom wearing a silver knee-length dress that clings to her flawless body. Her golden hair is curled and falling over her bare shoulders. She's breathtaking.

I don't look too bad myself. I managed to find a black mini-skirt and matched it with a black tank top and open-toed mules.

On the drive to Nanaimo, I slide a blues CD into the stereo. Ava sings along, occasionally changing her voice to make me laugh. By the time we reach the restaurant, the constant sadness I've felt since Dad died is lifted and for the first time in weeks, I feel hope that things are going to be alright.

We order the most expensive things on the menu: ribeye steaks, lobster, and a couple glasses of their best wine. When we're finished eating, Ava leans across the table and grabs onto my hand. "I'm crazy about you," she says.

"I feel the same way." I smile. "Thank you for being there for me while I was going through my bad time."

"Ditto," she says. "You were there for me, too."

"I know I haven't been too attentive to you lately. I'm sorry about that. I guess I've been in a funk, but I think I'm finally starting to snap out of it."

"Take your time. Don't rush what you need to go through. It's a process."

"Thank you." I kiss her hand. "But I want to know how you're feeling, too. Is there anything bothering you lately? Have you heard from your siblings over the past few weeks?"

"No. I haven't heard anything. I had a moment of worry the other day—I was waiting outside of the bank for you and I could've sworn I saw Cliff. But when he got closer, I saw that it wasn't him."

"Are you expecting him to show up again? Or do you think he gave up and left town?"

She scoffs. "Cliff would never give up on anything he wanted. Especially money. I think he's still somewhere close, biding his time, waiting for me to come up with the cash."

"Well, you know him better than anyone. You're not still thinking of selling your car to pay him off, are you?"

"What choice do I have? I wrote the ad up today. I am going to list it in the classifieds tomorrow."

"I am not going to let you do that. Plus, even if it does sell, you'll still be five grand short."

Ava sighs. "It's a start."

I squeeze her hand and look deep into her eyes. "I want to give you the money, and I don't want to hear a word about it."

"No, Mila—"

"You said it yourself. We're together, and what happens to one of us, happens to both. I want to pay Cliff off so he goes away and stays gone. You won't have to worry about him anymore, and I won't have to worry about your safety."

A tear streams down her face. "It's a lot of money, Mila. It would take me ages to pay you back."

"It'd be a gift, not a loan."

"Are you sure?"

"Positive."

She gets up and walks around the table, then leans down and kisses me. "I love you so much."

After dinner, we go to the theatre and sit in the back row. When the flick starts playing and the lights dim, Ava and I can't keep our hands off each other. Things quickly escalate and before we know it, people are starting to turn around and stare. Giggling, we leave the movie early and decide to go back to the cabin where we can be alone.

Ava teases me on the drive home, her playful hands running over me, causing me to swerve on the road. By the time I park in front of the cabin, both of us are heated and hungry for one another.

We're both laughing as she undoes my shirt and I fumble with the key in the door. As soon as we're inside, our lips meet, and we stumble towards the bedroom, not even stopping to turn on the lights.

We're almost to the bedroom when Ava pulls away. "I'll be right back," she whispers, and I watch her dark silhouette head for the bathroom. She flicks on the light, and the living room is illuminated enough for me to see something on the couch. Something that wasn't there when we left.

I quickly go to the floor lamp and click it on.

There, wrapped in a purple fuzzy jacket and fast asleep on the sofa, is Jessica.

"What is it?" asks Ava, standing in the washroom doorway.

"It's your sister."

"You're kidding," she says, running over to take a look. "Jessica!" Ava pushes on her sister's shoulder.

Jessica groans and blinks a few times. "Hey, sis. How've you been?"

"How did you get in here?" I demand.

Jessica smiles. "You left the window unlocked."

Rage instantly boils up in me.

"Where have you been?" Ava's voice crackles with emotion. "I've been worried sick."

Jessica sits up and Ava sits beside her. The smile slides off Jessica's face when she takes a good look at Ava. "Oh my God! What happened to your face?"

"It's a long story," Ava says, starting to cry.

Jessica grabs onto her sister and hugs her tightly. "Everything's going to be okay, Ava."

"Ava, I'm going to go into the bedroom," I say, with that familiar feeling of being a third wheel. "I'll let you guys talk, okay?"

In my room, I sit on the bed, feeling a sense of uneasiness over Jessica being here. I don't trust her as far as I can throw her. Not to mention, she's an arsonist and

228

most likely a killer, too. I listen intently as the two girls talk in the other room.

"I'm sorry I left without talking to you first, Ava. I was feeling crazy after being in prison and I kind of went rogue for a while."

"Where did you go?"

Jessica tells her how she went to Vancouver and got lost in the party scene for a while and how she's done with that lifestyle now. (*Yeah, right!* I think to myself.) Ava mentions that the parole office issued a warrant, that the police came by, and Jessica says that she wants to get clean before turning herself in because, apparently, "prison is the last place you want to be when going through withdrawal."

I'm not sure if it's Ava's strategy to keep Jessica from running again, but the subject of the fires hasn't come up.

"Tell me what happened to your face, Ava," Jessica demands.

"I had just gotten home from playing a gig in Nanaimo," Ava says, "and out of nowhere, Cliff showed up and beat the hell out of me. He wanted money because he owes some gang bangers ten grand. He's desperate, Jess. I'm really worried. He's worse now than he ever was."

"Oh, God. This is bad, Ava." Jessica pauses. "But don't worry about it, okay? I'm going to fix things. I promise."

Why doesn't Ava mention Cliff's video showing Jessica at the scene of the fire? I tell myself that Ava knows best, but I'm still uneasy about the whole thing.

"You don't have to fix anything. I can get him the money."

"You have access to ten g's?" Jessica sounds shocked.

"Mila's father died and left her a lot of money. She said she'll give me what I need to pay off Cliff."

"Oh. Well, anyway, let's not worry about all that. What I really want to know is if you're doing okay. How have you been feeling?"

"I feel great, all things considered. I've been writing quite a few new songs. They're good. I think you'd like them. If you want me to play for you tomorrow, I can."

"I'd love that," Jessica replies. "Have you been taking your pills?"

"Of course, I have. Why do you ask?" Ava's tone is defensive.

I can't believe how motherly Jessica is being. *It's an act,* my brain says immediately. *She's trying to fool Ava into thinking she cares about her.*

"I only ask because I love you, silly. You're my baby sis."

By the time Ava finally comes to bed, I'm in my nightie and almost asleep. She cuddles in beside me and whispers softly in my ear, "I love you."

* * *

230

Despite my skepticism, things have been different with Jessica over the past week. She's not as radical and offensive. Both she and Ava have spent the past week walking on the beach, going to town, and reconnecting. It's the first time I can imagine them as children with an honest and mutual admiration for each other.

Jessica hasn't been as catty with me, like she was the first time she stayed. She even invited me to participate in different things her and Ava were doing.

The girls went to the doctor in town and got a prescription to help Jessica while she detoxes from the alcohol and street drugs she was taking. There have been a few nights where Ava got out of bed to massage her sister's legs, which ached from the withdrawal. Apparently sugar helps when coming off drugs too, which explains all the candy wrappers lying around.

Today, Ava has planned for the three of us to go to Nanaimo to buy seafood from the boats on the dock. Afterwards, there's apparently a "fun surprise." I'm just praying it's not bungee jumping or something equally crazy.

I'm awake before Ava, so I decide to go to the kitchen and make a pot of coffee for everyone. I quietly open the door and when I tiptoe out of the bedroom, my eyes immediately focus on the neatly folded blanket on the couch.

The bathroom door is open, so I know Jessica isn't in the shower. It briefly occurs to me that she probably awoke early and went for a walk on the beach, until I see the note lying on the table.

As I walk up to the table, a sense of dismay comes over me and before I even pick up the note, I know that whatever is written on it will devastate Ava. As much as it's not in my character to read a letter addressed to someone else, I need to know what Jessica wrote so I can help Ava later. I pick up the one-page note.

Ava, I can't keep doing this. I love you completely and the whole time I was in prison, I worried about you. Since I've been out, I thought I could control things but I can't. It's obvious that I've failed you and I will always be sorry for that. I have gone to find Cliff to sort things out so you'll be okay in the future. But I can't go back to jail, Ava. I just can't. I deserve to have a life regardless of the mistakes I've made. Don't hate me. I'll see you soon. Love, Jess.

I sigh deeply and set the note back down on the table. This isn't good. Ava will be heartbroken that Jessica decided not to turn herself in, especially after so many days of helping her detox. This news will completely destroy Ava.

I don't make coffee. I don't want to create any noise that could wake her. It's not like we'll be heading to Nanaimo this morning as planned, so it's best to let her sleep as long as possible. I quietly get a glass of water and sit on the couch to wait.

An hour passes before I hear rustling coming from the bedroom, and a sinking feeling hits my stomach. A few moments later, Ava walks into the living room and smiles when she sees me. "Good morning, beautiful." I force a smile. On her way to the washroom, she looks around. "Where's Jess?"

"I don't know."

"What do you mean?"

I point to the table. "She left you a note."

Her face drops as she reads. Her expression changes from confusion to hurt.

"How could she do this?" She crumples the paper in her hand and drops it back on the table. "She promised me that she'd finish getting clean and then turn herself in. I'm such a fool for trusting her again."

I stand and walk over to her, putting a hand on her shoulder. "It's not your fault, and you're not a fool. Just a caring person who tried to help her sister."

With tears in her eyes, Ava goes back into the bedroom, re-emerging with her cell phone in hand. She calls Jessica and leaves a message, pleading for her to come back so the two of them can talk things out. When she's done the call, she walks over to the couch and collapses in tears.

Sitting next to her with my hand on her back, I know there's nothing I can do to ease her pain. Just like me after my father's death, this is something she has to work through in her own time.

* * *

Over the next four days, it's almost impossible getting Ava to eat anything. All she does is pace the floor until she gets tired, then she goes into the bedroom and shuts the door.

It's almost midnight on day four, and Ava has been walking around like a zombie all day. I've got to do something to reconnect with her if I'm going to try pulling her out of her depression.

I grab her brush from the bathroom counter. After some convincing, Ava sits on the floor while I sit on the couch behind her. I begin gently brushing her long hair. I talk about the garden she wants and how someday we'll have one. Then, I describe a cozy house where we'll live one day. How in the house, there'll be a wonderful music room for her to write and play her songs in.

Suddenly, she wraps her arms around my legs and holds on tightly. "Promise me we'll always be together?"

"I promise."

Just then, there's a light tap at the door.

Ava jumps up. "It's Jessica," she says excitedly. "It has to be."

She quickly unlocks the door and swings it open. Then, as if she's seeing a ghost, she slowly backs up.

An eerie feeling comes over me. I watch as Jessica walks into the light of the entrance way. Then, from behind her, someone's arm comes out of the darkness and pushes on the door.

A large man steps into the light. It's Cliff, looking more devilish and creepy than when I first saw him.

She betrayed Ava.

I've got to protect Ava.

Before I can think, I'm running into the bedroom and throwing open the closet. From its depths I pull out my father's shotgun.

I quickly check to see if it's loaded. Not surprisingly, it is. My mom used to get so upset with Dad for keeping his guns loaded. His gruff voice echoes in my memory. *"If a burglar breaks in, I need to be ready."*

As I walk out of the bedroom, my hands are shaking so badly, I'm afraid of dropping the gun. The first thing I see is Ava, cowering in the corner of the room. Then I see Cliff and Jessica slowly approaching her.

"Stop right there," I scream, leveling the gun at them, "or I'll blow your fucking heads off."

Everyone turns and sees me standing with the gun. Jessica and Cliff freeze in their tracks.

"Come over here, Ava," I holler.

She looks at her siblings, then quickly sprints across the floor and hides behind me.

"Mila, you don't understand," Cliff says. "We didn't come to hurt her, we came to talk to her."

"Oh yeah, sure," I retort. "Just like you came over here before and beat her senseless when she got out of her car?"

"I never hit her. I would never hurt my sister. And this is my first time here. I didn't even know where you lived until now."

"Don't listen to him, Mila," Ava says from behind me, her voice trembling. "He's lying,"

"I don't believe you," I tell Cliff. "The first time I met you, in the cab, you tried to intimidate me with a knife."

"Yes, I did. When I found out your name and that you drove cab, I wanted to check you out and, yeah, to intimidate you a little. Ava is our little sister, and I wanted you to know that I was here to protect her, no matter what."

"You never said you were her brother."

"No. I wasn't sure if she'd told you about me yet. I was leaving that to her."

"You know what?" I raise the gun a fraction. "I don't give a shit about that. I just want the both of you to get the hell out of here and leave Ava alone."

"You've been lied to, Mila," he insists. "Isn't that right, Ava?"

Ava says nothing. I glare at Cliff. "What about the money you're trying to get from her? You threatened to reveal what Jessica did if Ava didn't pay."

Jessica steps forward. "He did want money from Ava. He was in a bad spot. But it wasn't me he was threatening to expose."

"Why are you doing this, Jess?" Ava cries.

"I would never listen to you, Jessica," I snarl. "You're a fucking criminal and a druggie. Not to mention, you're responsible for a man's death—"

"Jessica went to jail, yes," Cliff interrupts. "But only because she didn't want Ava to be locked up in her condition. She knew Ava wouldn't last a day behind bars, so she confessed to crimes she never committed so Ava could be free."

"Liar!" Ava screams, and I jump. "You are both liars!"

Tears are now streaming down Jessica's face. "I love you Ava," she says, her voice breaking. "But I can't do this anymore. I just can't. You need help."

My heart is racing and my head is spinning. "I'm only asking you one more time. Get the hell out."

"Will you just look at something?" Cliff says, taking a step toward us. "I promise we will leave. But just watch one thing—"

"Stop right there," I yell. "I mean it. Take another step and I'll blow your legs off."

"Make them go away," Ava whimpers.

Cliff puts his hands in front of him, then slowly backs up. Then he takes a phone out of his pocket. He crouches down and slides it across the floor toward me. "Please, just hit the play button on the first video."

"Go away," Ava screams. "Go away."

I find myself drawn to the phone on the floor. "Ava, everything is going to be okay. Don't worry. I just have to look at the video and they'll leave."

"No!" Ava cries, sounding terrified. "Why are you doing what he says? He's trying to trick you."

"The phone isn't going to hurt me. Here–" I hand Ava the gun. "Keep it pointed at Cliff."

I step toward the phone, which stopped only a foot away from where I'm standing. Keeping a wary eye on the other two, I kneel down and pick up the phone. I slide the bar across the screen to open it. It's already in the image gallery, with a video already cued up. I tap the play button.

At first, all I see is a dark forest. A few seconds later, I see flames. They seem to be coming from the bottom window of a small building.

Then, there's a flash from headlights. A car backs up into view, and in the light of the dashboard, I see a blond woman wearing a purple sweater driving.

I feel, suddenly, sick. *It can't be. It's someone else.*

The camera follows the car through the trees. As soon as I see the taillights and licence plate, I gasp and drop the phone.

It's her. Ava.

"Ava, put the gun down," Jessica suddenly cries.

I stand and turn to see Ava with a crazed look on her face. The barrel of my father's shotgun is pointed at me.

"What the hell is going on here, Ava?" My legs are weak with fear.

"She needs help, Mila. She's very sick. If you love her, you will–" Cliff's words are cut short as the barrel of the gun shifts from me to him, and the thunderous boom of the shotgun blasts through the cabin.

My ears ring so loudly that I can barely hear the blood curdling scream coming from Jessica. I watch her leap across the floor and land on top of Ava, knocking the gun to the floor.

Everything is moving in slow motion as I turn my head to see Cliff's body slumped over on the floor, an explosion of blood on the wall where he was standing just a few seconds ago.

I'm not sure if Jessica called the police, or if a neighbour who heard the blast did, but soon, the cabin is lit up with flashing lights shining through the windows.

Chapter Sixteen

There was no funeral for Cliff. Just a write up in the paper stating that a man had been shot and was pronounced dead on scene.

Remarkably, Ava was never mentioned as the person who started the house fires that killed a man near the Nanaimo River. There was only a short write-up stating that police had solved the case.

Some time ago, Jessica mailed me a letter. It said that she is doing well, has been clean and sober for over a year now, and is living in Victoria. She's working at a community center, helping other addicts get their lives back.

She mentioned how she sees Ava every week at the institution, how Ava is like a zombie some days but when she has clear moments, she asks about me. Ava says in these moments that I'll always be her one true love. In the course of interrogations and interviews by the police, then later while attending court, I learned that Ava suffers with an array of mental illnesses. Bi-polar disorder, PTSD, and borderline personality disorder. I'm still amazed at how well she kept it together when she was around me. The Olanzapine, a heavy antipsychotic medication, helped.

However, she still had episodes that she couldn't control. That's when she lit the fires and came up with the elaborate tales about Jessica and Cliff.

I still can't believe that I never detected anything odd in her behavior. I was so in love. I only saw her through rose-colored glasses.

* * *

Majestic waves rise up from the open sea and crash onto large, jagged rocks on shore.

Today is my first day working at the whale watching office in Tofino. I plan on saving enough money so maybe, in the future, I can continue my education to become a teacher. The inheritance Dad left me paid the down payment on a cottage just steps away from the beach. Next to the door hangs a handmade shell mobile.

The little community is peaceful and has a wonderful, welcoming vibe. Full of artists. Ava would've been in heaven here.

As I walk up the wooden ramp to the office, I briefly close my eyes. For a split second, I'm transported back to when she and I were here together.

I remember how she leaned over in the boat, and her sweet voice whispers in my memory.

"I love you."

The End

Readers we need you.

Please leave a review, even a one liner counts, and has a big influence on our future sales.

Also published by BWL Publishing Inc.

Hush
Shatter
Shiver
Storm
The Cove
Impulse
The Immoral

BWL Author
Jay Lang

Jay Lang grew up on the ocean, splitting her time between Read Island and Vancouver Island before moving to Vancouver to work as a TV, film and commercial actress. Eventually she left the industry for a quieter life on a live-a-board boat, where she worked as a clothing designer for rock bands. Five years later she moved to Abbotsford to attend university. There, she fell in love with creative writing and wrote five novel manuscripts in a year. She spends her days hiking and drawing inspiration for her writing from nature.

BWL Publishing

bwlpublishing.ca